THE AIR BETWEEN US

The Air Between Us

An Erotic Romance

SHAMEKA S. ERBY

Shameka S. Erby

Cover design by: The Chary Assist
ISBN: 979-8-9904265-0-4
Printed in the United States of America

Dedication

To first loves that never die, and new loves who make room. And to all my fine ass fat girls getting fucked properly--you deserve!

Content Warning

Biphobia, gunplay, violence, death, miscarriage (past), neglectful parents, and mentions of drug use

Author's Note

This is a polyamorous, closed triad, erotic romance. One of the characters has a past with one love, and a present with the other so it will be fast paced and full of sex. They get it in--a lot. And there are fluid exchanges aplenty. These people are squirting, spraying and swallowing. Just so you know. But it's still gentle and sweet. Because I am gentle and sweet :)

Chapter 1

Trevino "Truck" Davis

In the dead of night, a watchful shadow, the most danger-ous ghost, settled over the road where the drop was taking place. He was out of sight, but with a reputation like his, he was never out of mind. He was perched high, looking low, lethal in every way. As two cars approached each other, he took a deep breath. The shadow centered himself, thought of home, knew he was close to being there.

The cars stopped, their headlights bouncing off each other. A pair of men exited the backseat of each vehicle, two of the four men carrying a duffle bag. In the distance, leaves rustled in the wind, sweeping through the clearing and startling everyone. All four men jumped back, guns drawn.

"Easy," the ghost whispered, his words drifting into his earpiece, "it was just the wind. You're good, cuzzo. Be easy."

The man who heard his assurance straightened his shoulders and got back to business. Words were exchanged and bags were traded; the drop was done. But before anyone could return to their cars, another one pulled up, this one full of armed men ready to take out King, the man with an earpiece connection to the ghost.

The ghost was Trevino "Truck" Davis, the deadliest enforcer anyone had ever known, the quietest threat in this corner of the world, and he was almost insulted these niggas thought they could roll up on his cousin with no repercussions. He aimed his sniper rifle at the car. Three seconds later, three of the five men who'd exited the car were on the ground. Three seconds more and the two men who'd made the exchange were on the ground too, while everyone else was firing wildly and scrambling for cover.

Truck chewed his strawberry gum, focused his scope, knocked off one more. His cousin was back in his protected vehicle with both bags, waiting for the all-clear. Two more shots rendered the drivers of the two enemy cars dead, and his cousin's men grabbed up the one man who was left and took care of him.

"Code 4, cuzzo," he said softly, putting his rifle down and starting to disassemble it. "I'm out."

"Watch your body, my nigga," his cousin, Romelo "King" Davis said back. There was a moment of static, then the earbud went dark. Truck removed it and put it in his pocket. He took his bagged rifle and got down from his sniper perch, moving through the shadows to his car. Taking the earbud out, he smashed it under his boot. Then he wrapped the mangled pieces in his gum, dropped the wad in an old water bottle with a little bleach at the bottom, and tossed the bottle into a nearby dumpster. He removed the tarp he'd covered the car with and got in, driving away.

Thirty minutes later, Truck typed the code on the keypad at his front door. He entered the house and dropped his bag on the bench in the entryway. The open floor plan greeted him with high ceilings and the muted but warm tones of the walls and furniture. Crossing the room, he walked into the kitchen, grabbing a water and a wrapped package he knew was a smoked turkey and Swiss cheese sandwich, then went to his bedroom, putting them down on the table in the sitting area. Truck undressed and headed to the en suite bathroom, showering quickly and coming out again. He sat naked in one of the comfortable club chairs in the sitting area, devouring the sandwich and drinking his water. Then he climbed into bed. No sooner than he was settled, a pair of arms wrapped around him from behind.

"Good morning, Trev," the sleepy voice of his lover rumbled in his ear. Truck smiled. Everything was normal again.

"Good morning, Butta," he said, using his special nickname for the man beside him. Bashir Rosewood, also known as Bash in the neighborhood and "Butta" to him and him only, had been his man, his lover, and his other half for the last five years. Being a bisexual man wasn't exactly a hindrance to a nigga like Truck—his reputation meant no one dared question anything he did. In fact, his street persona only made women *and* men want him more, although most of them would rather die than admit it. The women tended to be more openminded, but there was still bigotry. Even still, he never thought he'd fall in love...not again, anyway. Bashir Rosewood changed everything.

When Bash came out, people tried him every way they could. Bash was a fighter, in the literal sense—a trained amateur welterweight, to be exact—so he fought everyone who had a derogatory thing to say. Then one day, something compelled Truck to step in.

Maybe it was Bash wiping the blood off his full bottom lip, getting into his fighter stance as many times as it took; maybe it was the sight of his skill and stamina on display. Maybe it was his sexy ass beard and those deep brown eyes.

Who knows? All Truck knew was one day, he was tired of people acting like bitches, so he put his gun to the head of Bash's latest adversary. He told him and everyone else Bash was to be left alone—permanently.

Bashir hated it at first, insisted he could fight his own battles. Then Truck told him,

"I can't kiss you if your lip is always swollen, Butta. You gotta chill."

"What did you call me?"

"Butta. I like it. I think it fits you. It'll be my name for you."

"Listen, Truck—"

"Please, call me Trevino. Truck is a persona; these mufuckas call me that cause they don't know me. And I don't want them to. I do want you to know me, though. If you want to."

"Why do you want me to know you? Why do you want to know me?"

"I like a nigga who can stand up for himself. I don't want you bruising those hands no more, though. I like them too," Trevino said.

Bashir smiled, and it was like the sun coming out. Then he stared at him dubiously.

"I know you're bi, but these women throw themselves at you left and right. You ever even been with a dude before?" Bashir questioned.

Trevino smirked. "If you wondering how the dick work, we gotta build up to that, Butta. I ain't no easy nigga."

His last statement made Butta laugh and agree to grab dinner with him. They'd been together ever since. Bashir knew everything about Trevino, every flaw, every fear, every perceived failing. He was the one place the enforcer could lay his soul bare, and one of the few people Trevino trusted.

He turned in bed, kissed Bashir's forehead. Moments later, he was asleep.

The dream always started the same. Trevino was running, trying to catch up to her, trying to stop her.

"Nas, come back!" he was screaming, but she couldn't hear him.

Trevino sped up, tried again. He needed her to at least turn around, see his face. She was the only person he'd ever loved. He had to tell her. Trevino had to let her know she'd always have his heart, and she could find shelter with him whenever she needed it. If she was going to leave, she should at least know he'd always have a home for her. He ran faster.

"Nas, you can come to me, baby. You can always come to me," he yelled after her. Suddenly she stopped, turned, reached for him—

Trevino sat up in bed, covered in sweat, gasping for breath. He shook his head like he was trying to clear his thoughts. The dream was dissipating, as they often did, and only various stray images remained. But one thing was clear. The dream was about Nasima. He was confused and a little annoyed. Nasima Jones was long gone. What the hell was he doing dreaming about her again?

Nasima "Lil Baby" Jones

Nasima Amara Jones sat up in bed, throwing her legs over the side and taking a deep breath. She grabbed her leggings from the bottom of the bed and slid them on, putting her feet in the furry slippers on the floor below her and standing up.

After a few minutes of stretching, she grabbed her shower caddy and went to her room door, unlocking it and stepping into the hallway. The noise sounded like everyone was downstairs, so she ran into one of the two bathrooms in the hallway and shut the door. Nasima used the bathroom, brushed her teeth, washed and moisturized her face and then came out, going back into her bedroom. She put on a sports bra under her shirt—her titties seemed to have a mind of their own, and the last thing she needed was Tone getting the wrong idea. Then she headed downstairs. Everyone was in the living room, watching TV and being loud for no reason at eight a.m.

"'Bout time you got your ass down here. We hungry as shit," her cousin Smoke complained. Nasima scowled. She paid her rent on time. This cooking shit was extra, and the last thing she needed was grief about it.

"Good morning to you, too," she said with attitude.

"Good morning, Nas. Girl, don't mind him. He's just cranky." Smoke's girlfriend Candace laughed and waved. Candace was as lazy as the day was long, but she was sweet, and she knew how to rein Smoke in before his mouth got him in too much trouble. Nasima could appreciate that.

"As usual," Nasima said under her breath, turning to go into the kitchen. She went to the refrigerator and started pulling out ingredients, sitting them on the counter. As she bent to get the pots she would need from the bottom cabinet, she heard a low whistle.

"Damn, Nas! That ass still fat, ain't it? You should let me see if it's still soft."

"Tone, please don't start. Why can't you say good morning like a normal person?"

"Good morning, Nasima. Can I have some pussy?" Tone said, full of unfounded arrogance.

Nasima turned to face him, wondering what she ever saw in him. Anton "Tone" Messer was rude and surly with no ambition, and his mouth wrote checks neither his fists nor his dick could cash. He was a taker, through and through, and the fact that she'd gotten stuck with him here after throwing him out of her home was the cruelest twist of fate she'd ever known. Well, besides having to come back here in the first place.

"Tone, I wouldn't give you somebody else's pussy. Why won't you give it up? There's no more us, and you know why."

"You throwing me out was some bullshit and you know it. That's why you ended up right back here with me. You might as well stick it out with me. It don't get no better for bit—women like you. I'm your best bet," he said, opening his arms and shrugging his shoulders.

Nasima shook her head, holding her tears and anger at bay. Smoke wouldn't like it if she went off on his best friend, and she needed the room she was staying in, at least for now.

"I don't think that's true. Do you want cheese in your eggs?" she said, turning her back on him again. Nasima wanted to finish breakfast and go back up to her room to start working. After everything fell apart, she'd lucked into some remote data entry work, which gave her enough money to pay her cousin for his guest room. But besides her rent, Smoke took advantage of her culinary skills and put her in charge of the meals for the house. She was expected to feed everyone—even her ex-boyfriend.

Tone grumbled under his breath. "You gon learn one day, Nas. And yes, I want cheese in my eggs," he said, stomping out of the kitchen.

Nasima sighed and started cracking eggs. She didn't know what he was so sure she would learn, but if it had anything to do with taking him back, it was a lesson he could keep.

After breakfast, Nasima was able to sneak back up to her room and lock the door. She got on her laptop, checked on some better-paying jobs, then logged in to see her assignments for the day. There were only three, and none of them were terribly complicated. She'd have a good portion of the day to herself. Her contract meant her daily pay rate would be the same, whether she had two jobs or ten, so that was a small blessing.

Three hours later, she was dressed and leaving, her work finished and her room double-locked. Everyone was still home, but no one expected her to make lunch because she was usually working. Nasima walked down the street, heading to the avenue where everyone was usually posted up. She thought of treating herself to lunch, but small luxuries seemed wasteful when she was on a mission. She had to get out of here—again. She'd done it once, with the help of the only man who ever loved her, and then years of work crumbled when she fell for Tone, a man who'd probably never loved anyone.

Nasima decided to get a coffee and a sweet treat instead of a whole lunch and walked faster, using her favorite shortcuts to get to the Diner. As soon as she turned out of the alleyway, her heart stopped. She almost tripped over her own feet, the world shrinking to this moment. All she could see was him. Trevino Davis was posted up in front of the Diner, flexing with his shiny classic car, leaning into the second-finest man she'd ever seen as they laughed over some private joke. Nasima knew she would run into him eventually, but being in the moment was almost too much.

She focused on the other man, attempting to gather herself, but he didn't make it easier.

The man standing next to Trevino was his man, Bashir. Everyone knew Bashir, and everyone knew trying him would turn Trevino into Truck real quick. Even her cousin and Tone kept their homophobic jokes and comments to the house where there was no chance of it getting back to the streets. Bashir was a fighter, though, she'd heard. And fine as hell. He was light skin with hints of warm undertone, ginger hair, and big brown eyes. His mustache and full beard were a throne for the right person, the perfect seat with his fleshy lips and wide nose. He was larger-bodied than Trevino, a teddy bear almost, his stocky build making her want to cuddle. But they were about the same height, six-foot giants compared to her five foot three.

Trevino was still as beautiful as she remembered—smooth walnut skin, a wiry, muscular body, long ass arms and legs. His full mouth was still kissable, suckable, his hooded eyes still dark and penetrating. She couldn't see his arms or chest, but she knew they were covered in tattoos.

It was him. Trevino Davis. The only man who'd ever loved her. The man who helped her escape the first time.

Bashir "Butta" Rosewood

Bashir Jamal Rosewood loved Trevino Davis long before the day he told the streets he was off-limits and asked him out. He was a man you couldn't help but love. But Bashir saw something different than everyone else.

To most people, Trev's allure was his darkness and mystery. Everyone knew he was King's cousin, and though no one said it out loud, his enforcer. Everyone knew Truck could make you disappear. They were attracted to his silent deadliness, his toughness, his ability to fill you with hot lead and stay ice-cold. But Bashir knew his heart. He knew Trevino was really in the business of protection. He knew as far as blood, Romelo was all Trev had in the world, and he'd shed blood to protect him, right or wrong.

Bashir knew *that* was his real motivation. It wasn't violence, or mastery, or even reputation. Truck Davis existed to keep this corner of the world safe for the only family he had left. Loyalty and love were all Bashir saw, and what he fell in love with.

His relationship with Trev was passionate and safe, free and unapologetic. He had no problem telling him any and everything. Trevino was a provider who wanted to do for the people around him, make sure they were okay. Bashir knew he was spoiled. But he wanted to spoil Trev too, and he knew the way to do it was to find their missing piece.

As solid and satisfying as their relationship was, they both agreed on the feeling that deep down, they were meant to be three. They'd tried bringing another person in twice before—another man first, a woman second—but those involvements turned into complicated competitions and displays of insecurity. Both of them had treated the relationship like a battle for him and Trev's love or a game they needed to win, instead of trusting Bashir and Trevino's promise of everyone getting everything they needed.

But he wasn't giving up, especially since Trevino had started dreaming of Nas again. Bashir knew the dreams were Trev's subconscious telling him she was closer than he knew. Trev didn't believe it, though.

And now they were standing in front of the Diner, enjoying the cold air and showing off their restored 1963 Corvette. Trev was telling him a dirty joke, and he was enjoying his man's warm breath in his ear as much as he was wait-ing for the punchline. He loved Trevino like this, laughing and relaxed. Bashir chuckled, then his spine tingled with awareness.

Something told him to look up. He did, and his gaze clashed with a pair of whiskey eyes. She was staring at them, appreciating them, admiring them. Bashir drew in a breath, took in her entire face. This was Nasima. The woman in Trev's dreams. The one he'd helped escape from here, and the only person, outside of Romelo and Bashir himself, that Trevino ever loved.

Bashir took a minute to look at her, appreciating her in return. She was a short woman, but very round. Her belly bulged, her hips and waist spread wide to uphold it, and her thighs were shaped like ham hocks. Bashir loved ham hocks. Her titties sat up, like she had on a good bra, but they were big and bouncy, barely behaving under her shirt. Her tawny skin had some copper to it, but she looked tired and a little scared, which dimmed her light a bit. Bashir found himself wanting to eliminate whatever and whoever was making her look so...defeated. She had a pert little nose and elfin ears, and her highlighted hair had been thrown into a haphazard ponytail. Those soulful, whiskey eyes were sad, and her full mouth trembled like she was seconds from tears. She was breathtaking, and Bashir wanted her in his arms with an urgency that nearly frightened him.

He nudged his man, urged his eyes in the right direction. Trevino's gaze found Nasima, and he gasped. His hands shook, and Bashir could feel his breath speeding up. It's her, he thought. She's our missing piece...because he still loves her.

Trevino

Trevino responded to Butta's nudge and looked up.

His heart stopped; the world stopped. Nasima Jones was standing at the entrance to the alleyway, staring at him and Bashir like she wanted to absorb into them. When he lost Nasima, when he sent her away, she was young—they both were. But she was a woman now, a full-grown goddess. A fine ass fat mama with tawny skin and whiskey eyes. Her hair was shorter than he remembered from years ago, but still in the bouncy high ponytail she'd loved to wear since they were teenagers. He could tell she'd been through some things, but her face was still the same one burned into his memory and etched on his heart. And if looking into her eyes wasn't enough, her body was magnificent—bouncy belly, big titties, jiggly arms, soft folds, and thighs he knew would smother his dick and his face. She was the most beautiful thing he'd ever seen, and he realized why neither of the others he and Bash chose had worked out. Their real missing piece was standing in front of them, and Trevino knew he had to find a way to make her see it too.

"Nas? Is that you?" He was finally able to speak. Her smile was shy, small, like she was afraid to be happy to see him. Truck Davis the enforcer growled underneath, rising to the surface. Someone had hurt her—badly. There was no other explanation for the shadows in her eyes, the hesitance in her smile. Someone had taken her happiness, and as soon as he figured out who it was, they were dead.

"Not now," Bash whispered, calming him. "Focus on her now. Find that nigga later." His lover's words snapped him back into the moment, where Nasima was still standing in the alleyway, waving shyly.

"You better come here, Lil Baby," he said, sliding into his old nickname for her. Nasima smiled bigger and made her feet move. As soon as she was close enough, he pulled her into his arms. She molded to him, relaxed against him, sighing with a mix of relief and pleasure. Trevino rubbed her back and kissed the top of her head.

"Vino, I missed you," she said, dropping her nickname for him just as easily. She stepped back like she thought she wasn't supposed to hug him so tightly. Trevino almost laughed. Clearly, she knew about Bashir. He pulled her close again, turning her to face his lover.

"Lil Baby, this is Bashir, the person I love. Butta, this is Nasima—"

"The only other person you've loved. Nasima, you're gorgeous, and it's lovely to meet you," Bashir said, taking her hand and kissing it.

Nasima stared at him like she didn't know if it was appropriate to respond. She licked her lips.

"Um, thank you. You're very nice looking yourself, Bashir. It's good to meet you, and I appreciate you taking such good care of Vino. He's a protector, but he needs someone too."

"He does take good care of me. But I'm cool, Lil Baby, you know how I do. Forget about me, tell me what's going on with you. What are you even doing here?" Trevino said.

Nasima avoided his eyes, and her shoulders hunched, like she was putting up a wall around herself.

"It's kind of an embarrassing story, Vino—"

"Aye." He stopped her, lifting her chin so he could look into her eyes. "Ain't no such thing. You know there's nothing you can't tell me. Let's go in the Diner. You eat?"

She shook her head, and Trevino grabbed her and Bashir's hands, leading them inside the small neighborhood restaurant. He found a corner booth and sat down, making sure he was facing the door with his back to the wall. Nasima slid into the booth, but Bashir hesitated.

"I can let y'all be alone. I don't want you to feel like you need to hold back with Trev because I'm here," he said, directing the last part to Nasima. This time, her smile was genuine.

"You can stay. Vino trusting you is all I need to know," she said.

Trevino smiled, proud he was still her anchor and her compass. He'd taught her how to survive, then made her promise she'd never forget who she could count on. Bashir sat down, smiling as well.

The server came over, pen and pad in hand. "Y'all ready, Truck?" she said, addressing him the way the streets normally did. Trevino nodded.

"Yeah, Kat. We'll all have ice water and root beers. Then bring cheese fries for the table, onion rings, and three turkey clubs—Swiss cheese for me, American for these heathens."

The woman nodded and left the table. Butta and Nas looked at each other, sharing a smile and then a laugh.

"Not too much on American cheese," Nasima said.

Bashir nodded. "Tell 'em, Nas," he added, backing her up.

Trevino grinned. He liked seeing them connect, even if it was over something as simple as cheese. They sat in silence until three ice waters and three sodas made it to the table.

Trevino sipped his water, waiting. Nasima needed to tell him everything. As pleased as he was to see her, he knew life must have knocked Nas on her ass hard for her to even consider coming back here.

Nasima downed half the glass of water and wiped her mouth on a napkin. She looked between him and Butta, taking slow breaths. It was like the air was easier for her when she was between them. Trevino knew the feeling. The air was easier for him now too.

"Things were okay when I first left," Nasima said, folding her hands on the table. "I got the job, and I used the money exactly how you told me to. I lived well, and I was happy. As happy as I could be missing you, anyway."

"Lil Baby, you don't need to say that. I wouldn't be mad if you'd forgotten about me. I was a part of this place, and I would have understood wanting to wipe it from your memory," he rushed to reassure her. Nasima shook her head.

"You have no idea of the mark you leave, Vino. I wouldn't forget you even if I could. I missed you every day, but it was okay because I knew I was doing what we agreed to. Five years ago, I came home on a whim and ran into Tone. We got to talking, and he told me he was trying to get out of here too. I admired his focus, so I kept in touch with him. He visited me every other weekend like clockwork, and we got serious. After we'd been together about eight months, he said his brother was throwing him out, and I told him he could come and stay with me."

Nasima took a break to finish her water. Bashir was frowning, and Trevino knew it was because he was putting the pieces together in his mind.

"You came to see Trev, didn't you?" he finally said. Nasima nodded, not speaking.

Trevino scowled. "And let me guess, I'd just hooked up with Butta, and Tone made sure he told you so you wouldn't come to me."

Nasima nodded again, as ashamed as she'd been when she first realized Tone basically set her up. He took another sip of water, controlling his anger. It wasn't his Lil Baby's fault, and he wouldn't take it out on her. Butta sat back against the seat, controlling his anger too.

"Tone and I were okay, for the most part. He worked and helped with bills—not as much as I wanted, but he did. He had his ways, but I wanted to give him a chance. He was so insecure about our bond, Vino. He brought you up all the time. I thought if I tried harder to reassure him... It didn't work. It only made him feel justified. You became something he threw in my face when I would confront him about his behavior or disrespect. I was easing my way out of the relationship anyway, but I felt bad because I knew Tone didn't have anywhere to go but back here. I was stuck. Then, six months ago, I found out all his other shit was a smokescreen for his real disrespect."

"Here you go!" Kat interrupted with their food. She sat down two big platters with onion rings and cheese fries, then three plates with packed club sandwiches. She pulled some extra napkins from her apron pocket, gestured to someone to refill their waters, and floated away. Trevino used his fork to move a stack of onion rings and a pile of fries onto Nasima's sandwich plate. He made sure she was okay, then served himself. Bashir laughed softly, and Trevino knew he was showing his hand. But he couldn't help it. His Lil Baby was back, and she needed looking after.

"I know this is pissing Trev off cause it's pissing me off," Butta said, taking a huge bite of his sandwich, "but please tell us the rest. Trev needs to know everything."

"Are you sure, Vino? It's the past now, and I—"

"Tell me what he did, Nas," Trevino said, stuffing an onion ring in his mouth. Someone came with water refills, and they waited until she left. Nasima swallowed her food, nodding her head.

"My job downsized. They shifted me to part-time, and I had no choice but to accept it until I could find something else. When I went home to tell Tone, I found him with someone, some married woman who lived three floors above me. She ran out embarrassed, and I told Tone he needed to leave. Then I told the woman's husband. Two weeks later, I got a notice to vacate for violating the building's code of conduct. The woman snitched to management, telling them Tone wasn't on the lease and he was selling pills on the side. Apparently, she'd been getting dick and Percs from him. Others in the building corroborated the drug story, and I had to leave. With an eviction on my record and a part-time job, I wasn't going to get another apartment. I had nowhere to go but Smoke's house. And my luck kept getting worse because when I got here, I found out when I sent Tone packing, he had nowhere to go but Smoke's house his damn self." Nasima finished the story and went back to eating, her head down.

Trevino slid over and pulled her into his body, kissing the top of her head.

"Pick your head up, Lil Baby. You didn't do anything wrong. Come on, now. I got you now. Vino's here." He soothed her the way he had since they were kids. Nasima wrapped her arms around him and began to cry, her body shaking with sobs.

Butta stared at her, his gaze filled with sympathy and anger as he balled his fists. Trevino watched him turn into a warrior right before his eyes in defense of Nas, and it cemented his belief, his desire. She was the missing piece. The air between them.

Chapter 2

Bashir

Bashir moved closer to Nasima, rubbing her back as she cried into Trev's chest. His anger was close to exploding, and he needed to refocus on her to keep it at bay.

Trevino had shared everything about his past with Nasima, so he was aware of how alone she'd been in the world until Trev. He knew she was smart, kind, generous, and funny. He knew because his lover told him. The thought of anyone doing her dirty, especially someone she opened her home to, was making him want to lace on his gloves and fight.

Then there was his lover. He could feel the wrath coming off Trevino. Bashir thought of reasoning with him but changed his mind. He knew Truck Davis had been activated. His baby was patient, though. It wouldn't be tomorrow or the next day, but Tone had reached the end of his life and didn't know it.

"Nasima, thank you for telling us. Tone probably thought you'd be too embarrassed by what happened to come to us. And now that we know—"

"That nigga's days are numbered," Trevino finished, holding Nasima tighter. She sniffled, trying to get herself under control. After another minute, she pushed away, dragging her hand over her face.

"I'm sorry, Vino. I didn't mean to cloud how happy I am to see you with my bullshit. I'm okay. I have another job doing remote data entry, and I'm saving as much money as I can. I'll be right side up again soon, so don't worry."

"Lil Baby, I'm gonna excuse you for talking like this because you've been through a lot. But I know you know how I'm coming behind you. I'm gonna help you because I can and because I want to. Because I love you," Trevino said. He grinned at Bashir, and Bashir felt warm. Truck operated under the cover of darkness, but Trevino Davis was like the sun when he wanted to be.

Nasima looked between them, her gaze alarmed. "Vino, don't say that. Bashir—"

"Knows how much he loves you," Bashir jumped in. "We don't operate like immature people over here, Nasima. I'm secure in what we have. Trev hasn't shared his heart with many people. I would never begrudge him love or be petty and jealous when he gives me everything I need. I knew he loved you when I met him; I know he loves you now."

When he finished, Nasima stared at him, her whiskey eyes intrigued and full of interest. Bashir smiled. She was trying to figure him out. He'd left out the part where there was no need to be threatened by someone who was about to be his as well; he'd leave that for Trev.

"Butta is different, Lil Baby. And you'll figure out why on your own soon enough. Come on and finish eating. Then you can come to our house so I can take care of you. Got something to lay on you, too," Trevino said, nudging her plate back in front of her.

Nasima picked up her sandwich, taking a big bite. Her shoulders were relaxed now, her body settled. Bashir knew it was because she was relieved to have Trev fighting for her again. Little did she know she had two warriors now. Bashir refused to see anything else happen to her, refused to see the world take away her smile. Trev's story had painted a picture of her he wanted to know more about, and meeting her solidified his interest. He wanted Nasima—for him and Trev, and for himself.

The three of them finished eating and left. Trevino called a rideshare and sent him and Nasima ahead to the house, following behind them in the Corvette because it was a two-seater and he needed to make a stop. When they arrived, Bashir helped Nasima from the car and held her hand, taking her to the front door of their home—a three-story gray Victorian with turrets and a sloped roof, a second-story balcony, and bay windows.

"It's so beautiful," she whispered. Bashir smiled. He hoped she would love it.

"It was my Nana's house. We keep Trev's apartment on the West Side, but we needed a home. Come on, see the inside," he said. He punched in the door code and pushed inside, taking off his coat in the entryway and hanging it on a hook.

Nasima took off her coat as well and stood on her toes to put it on the hook next to his. Bashir grinned. Such a short, little fat mama. He was fascinated with her. Then he looked at her coat. Too skimpy for this weather and not high quality enough. He'd replace it soon.

Bashir took her hand again and led her into their open plan first floor. The kitchen was at the back and to the right, the family room beyond it. The living room was front and center, a bathroom off to the left. Beyond the bathroom was supposed to be dining space, but he and Trev never formally "dined," so it was a home gym, of sorts.

"You want to look around or sit with me?" he asked. Nasima turned to him, looking startled.

"We can sit. I want to wait for Vino," she said softly.

Bashir nodded and took her to the sectional. They settled next to each other, Nasima instinctively taking off her shoes so she could pull one of her legs underneath her. He loved seeing her get comfortable. He turned his body to face her, leaning close.

"Go ahead, ask me," he coaxed. Nasima gave him the same startled look.

"Ask you what?"

"I know you got questions, *Lil Baby*," he said, laughing as he tried out Trev's nickname for her. "You want to know if I'm jealous, how much I know about you and Trev, what he meant about me being different, what it's like being with grown man Trevino. You got hella questions. I can see them in those pretty ass eyes of yours."

"I didn't know if it was okay to ask," Nasima confessed. Bashir shrugged.

"Now you know it is. What do you want to know?"

"Vino has been this intense since the day I met him. It's good to see he hasn't changed. But I know he still works for King. Is he...okay?" she asked first. Bashir smiled. He hadn't expected her first question, but he loved it. It told him her heart was still as big as Trev remembered. He nodded.

"Yes, he's okay," Bashir assured her. "We don't talk about what he does—he won't pull me into the darkness with him because he loves me—but we talk about how he feels and why he does it. He works it out as best he can. My love is his balm, and his love is his redemption."

"Good. I'm happy you're not letting him hold it in. And I'm happy he's found someone who's stronger than I am. I used to worry so much, then I would worry my fear would knock him off his game. I was no good for him back then."

"You were perfect for him because you loved him," Bashir insisted, "and y'all were both young. King was still gathering territory, making his mark. The operation was all over the place. You were scared back then because you were supposed to be. There was a lot more to fear. It's much more of a well-oiled machine now."

"Thank you for saying that. Can I ask you...what's he like now? I know his hugs are still the same, but is everything else? Does he still sing horribly while he cooks and take water-wasting thirty-minute showers, and chew his nasty strawberry gum?" Nasima said.

Bashir burst into laughter. "Yes, yes, and yes. Trev is more focused now, and his skillset has increased tremendously. He's better than he's ever been—better reflexes, instincts. King is who he is because of how good Trev is. But outside of those things, he's the same. Hates wearing clothes in the house, leaves all his shit on the floor, craves fruit, not snacks when he's high. Same Trev."

"Oh, he's still leaving his shit everywhere? And the fruit! I used to get so annoyed with him. He won't touch a chip, cake, or donut, but he'll destroy three oranges, two bananas, and a pint of strawberries without even blinking!" Nasima said, laughing.

"A nigga can't be healthy?" Trevino said, walking in the door. Bashir turned, his eyes roving over his man, making sure he was all there. Then he smiled. They were all home.

Trevino

Trevino walked in his front door to the sound of laughter. Butta and Lil Baby were on the couch, sitting close, sharing jokes about him.

His heart sped up. This was how it was supposed to be—him coming off the grimy ass streets to his two loves. He hung up his coat, noticing Lil Baby's coat and making a note to replace it. He walked toward the couch, sitting on the other side of Nasima and rubbing her back. Now he needed the words to convince his Lil Baby.

"Healthy is leaving some fruit for somebody else, Vino," Nasima said, giggling while she answered his question. He smiled.

"I don't be thinking about it. I eat until I'm done eating," he said, shrugging. Bashir rolled his eyes, and Nasima giggled again.

"Keep going with your questions, Nasima," Bashir urged. Nasima leaned back a little, seeking his comfort, and he moved closer.

"Vino said you were different. How?" she asked. Bashir grinned and looked at him, his eyes asking if he wanted to take the lead on answering. Trevino nodded, breathing deep, which seemed to be easier to do when Nas was around.

"Listen, Lil Baby," he started, wrapping his arms around her, "me and Butta are solid. We love each other so much—"

She started squirming away from him.

"Of course, you do, Vino. I wasn't trying to—"

"Nas, hold on. Let me get this out," he said, pulling her back against him. He kissed her neck, knowing it would arouse her but settle her at the same time. "We love each other. But from the beginning, we've both felt like there was a missing piece. Like the two of us...were meant to be three."

"Three?" Nasima whispered. Trevino saw Bashir smile, and he nodded his head.

"Yes, three." Butta took over, grabbing Nasima's hands. "Twice before, we tried to fill that space. Twice before, it blew up in our faces. And when we saw you today, we knew the reason it never worked out. Our missing piece is you, Nas. We both believe that."

"We want you to be ours, Lil Baby. We want to be yours. Come home to love and be loved. We've been waiting a long time for you, baby," Trevino said, his voice low and shaking. Nasima couldn't reject them; he loved her too much to bear it.

She turned to face him, tears in her eyes.

"Vino, are you serious? I don't know how to do this. I'm not what you need. I don't want to hurt either of you because I'm inexperienced—"

"The point of this is teaching each other, Lil Baby. I want to be your man, your protector, your heart. And Butta wants to be the same. All we ask is for you to be open to learning us, loving us. I already know I'm in your heart. And I know once you learn Butta, you'll make room for him too. Our dynamic is an adjustment, and I don't take the learning curve for granted. But we can prove you belong with us if you give us a chance."

"We've been apart for so long. You don't know me anymore. Bashir doesn't know me at all. How can the two of you be so sure about this?" Nasima demanded.

Butta took her hands again, making her turn around and focus on him. "Trev shared your lives with me. He told me how you loved him, how you took care of each other. I believe you're still the person he loved, the person who helped him grow up. And meeting you only makes me want to know more. Let us date you, romance you, show you how niggas who care show up for you. Indulge in us, Nasima. I promise you won't regret getting to know me," he said.

Trevino grinned. Butta was one of a kind, and smooth as shit when he was ready to be. Nasima sighed and relaxed against him again.

"I don't think I'll regret it at all. I'm worried I won't be any good at this," she lamented.

"You don't have to be good, Lil Baby. You only have to be you. You fit in my arms, same as you always have. That's half the battle. I bet you fit in Butta's arms too," Trevino said, urging her forward.

Nasima turned to look at him again, biting her lower lip. Trevino nodded, encouraging her to follow her instincts. Because there was no way she didn't feel the pull when they were all together. Nasima gave him a small smile, kissed him softly. Then she turned back and threw her body forward. Butta caught her in his arms, and she straddled his lap. Nasima gripped his shoulders and buried her face in his neck.

"You smell so good," she whispered. Butta wrapped her in his big boxer arms and took the deepest breath.

"If you only knew how good it feels to hold you, Nas. The air is different; it's like I can breathe better."

"Really?" she asked, her voice going shy. Trevino frowned. His Lil Baby used to know her power. Tone's fumble was going to cost him his life, but first he was going to learn a very hard lesson about how to treat people who pour into you. Trevino moved over until he could put his arm around Bashir's shoulders. Nasima lifted her head, staring at the two of them.

"Tell me about your lives. I want to know what you do with each other, how you spend time together, everything," she said. Trevino grinned.

"We relax, a lot. Working with King keeps me stacked, and Butta owns the boxing gym where he used to train. He checks in three days a week, but it practically runs itself. We smoke, we love going out to eat, and we both love cars, so we buy a beat-up classic every six months or so and re-store it. Speaking of cars, I found a buyer for the Corvette, Butta."

"Word? That was fast," Bashir replied. He rubbed Nasima's back, and she put her head back down on his shoulder. "We also train together. Remember I told you Trev was more fo-cused, and his skillset had increased? It's because we spar together. Most of his work is gunplay, but boxing helps Trev work on his reflexes and listen to his instincts. It teaches him how to observe his opponent. Plus, the footwork helps him move quietly."

"You help him?" Nasima asked, surprised. Trevino knew her shock was from Bashir having the fortitude to partici-pate in his work in a way she couldn't, but he didn't blame her. He didn't want her anywhere near his work.

Bashir chuckled. "Hell yeah, I help. I need him to win. When he wins, he comes home. Every morning he walks back in here is another KO. Trev is undefeated, and I wanna keep him that way."

"I never thought of it like that. Maybe I can—"

"No, Lil Baby." He stopped her before she could finish her ridiculous suggestion. "I never wanted this to touch you. Butta is different from you, and I'm not expecting you to love me the way he does. I want *your* love; I don't want you to mimic his."

"Vino, when you tell me you want me the way you do, it's so impossible to say no."

"Don't you hate that shit?" Bashir said, lightening the moment. "He get to talking that slick shit and you give him anything he wants." He winked after he finished, and Trevino grinned.

"It's why he eats all the fruit and we don't say anything," Nasima said, joining the joke. The three of them laughed together.

"Look, Lil Baby, I'm not playing with you. I want you with us. But I know you need time. So how about a preview? Valentine's Day is two weeks from today. Come stay with us for two weeks. Let us show you who we are and how we can love you. Live with us so you can see firsthand how our dynamic works. Celebrate V-Day with us, then make your decision. Staying or going is always in your hands. I know you're gonna fall because no one is better at this than we are. But if you need to figure it out for yourself, give us two weeks to show you."

"What happens if I want to go after two weeks?" Nasima asked.

Trevino shrugged. "We'll still want to see you taken care of, so I'll get you a car—"

"And we'll put you in Trev's apartment," Bashir finished. Trevino nodded. Nasima shook her head.

"I couldn't let you—"

"It ain't up to you, Nas," Trevino cut her off. "You need your own space, and my apartment is roomy and safe. I'll still make sure you have everything you need. My love don't stop cause we ain't together. It hasn't stopped after all this time."

"Oh, Vino," she said, climbing from Butta's lap onto his. Trevino wrapped his arms around his Lil Baby, his gorgeous little fat mama, and knew he couldn't ever live without her again. He had two weeks to convince her she felt the same, two weeks to help her see Butta in the same light he did. It was a daunting task, but Trevino wasn't scared. If he could face off with unnamed enemies in the name of family, then he could bare his soul in the name of love.

Nasima went into quiet mode after, which was what he expected. Going from their reunion to opening up about what happened with Tone to getting asked to join their relationship was a lot for one day. He looked up at Butta, who nodded. Trevino got Nasima off his lap and back onto the couch. He kissed her forehead, and Butta did the same.

"We're gonna give you a minute, okay, Lil Baby? We'll be right in the kitchen. Come talk to us when you're ready," he said. Nasima nodded, giving him a small smile. The two men got up and went into the kitchen. Trevino grabbed two beers from the refrigerator, and Bashir pulled chips out of the cabinet. They sat at the table as Bashir opened their beers.

"You think we did too much? This is a lot right out the gate," he said, looking worried. Trevino sighed.

"It is a lot. But do you know how significant it was to see her today after constantly dreaming about her? When I was on my way to get her anyway?"

"I agree, Trev. And I can see in her eyes the idea intrigues her, but I don't want to overwhelm Nas. I want her to feel comfortable here," Bashir said. Trevino winked, taking a drink from his beer bottle.

"She will, and it will be because of you. You make it easy, Butta. You're the heart of this house," he said. Bashir smiled at him, and Trevino fell in love all over again. He leaned closer, and Bashir fed him potato chips, staring at him adoringly.

"You know, for such a dangerous guy, you are one romantic ass nigga," Bashir said, laughing.

Trevino grinned, shrugging his shoulders.

"What can I say? I got layers and shit," he said, joining his lover in laughter.

Nasima

Nasima took a deep breath, then another one. Trevino's proposition had her head spinning. The idea of those two fine, affectionate men wanting her in their lives, calling her their missing piece, was blowing her mind. Coming home had felt like failure, having to stay with Smoke felt like disaster, and being forced to see Tone every day was torture. So, two weeks away wasn't even something she had to think about.

But what about the rest? Could she open herself up to Vino and Bash? Could she be their girlfriend? Did she have enough love for them both? She had so many questions to pore over and even more to ask out loud.

Nasima got up from the couch where they'd left her and headed to the kitchen. The two of them were laughing together, eating chips and drinking beer. They looked so comfortable, so complete. Were they sure about there being room for her? It didn't look like they needed a single thing.

"Come sit with us and stop acting like an outsider," Trevino said.

"And stop thinking we don't need you," Bashir added, reading her mind. "We don't doubt ourselves in this house. We don't invite anyone here we don't have a place for."

Nasima smiled and sat down, properly chastised. Trevino got up and pulled a wine glass from the open shelving and a bottle from the refrigerator. He sat back down, pouring her a glass and pushing it over to her. Nasima took a sip, fortifying herself. She needed answers, although any questions about how well Trev knew her were out the window. They'd anticipated everything she wanted and needed today.

"You said you tried to find your third twice before. Why didn't it work?" she asked, jumping right in. The two men looked at each other, most likely trying to decide who could answer best. Trevino sighed.

"Our first try was another man. He was a good guy, smart and liked to have fun. But he was insecure when it came to me and Butta spending time alone. It was like he thought the addition of him was supposed to erase everything I felt for Butta separately. I couldn't give Bashir a kiss without giving him one too. Our workouts made him jealous, and working on the cars made him feel left out. We decided to find something he could do with each of us separately— you know, give him his own thing too. But he didn't want to try. He wanted us to stop everything we did together, point blank. I got his ass outta here," Trevino said, taking a drink after he finished.

Bashir smirked, patting Trevino's hand. Nasima took a long drink as he picked up the story.

"That nigga almost made Truck come out, which never happens in our home. It was a disaster. A year later, we met a lovely woman and decided maybe she could be the one. But where the guy was insecure, she was too competitive. Everything with her was about winning. Every time she got one of us to do something with her and not each other, she bragged. When we were out, she would be all over one of us and completely ignore the other, like she was trying to play us off against one another. It was over when she started telling people she had to teach us how to make a home and love each other. Acting like we were gorillas and she was civilizing us or some shit. I cut her loose while Trev was out working."

Trevino laughed after Bashir finished, and Nasima smiled as she sipped her wine. It seemed the two of them had a lot of adventures. She wanted to hear more stories, but it would have to wait. She needed to ask her questions.

"Will I have to sleep with you?" she asked. Trevino rolled his eyes.

"Man, have I ever had you in my home and not given you your own space? Next question, Lil Baby."

"I just thought—"

"We want to date you, Nas, not kidnap you. You won't be expected to sleep in our bed, or even sleep over here period, but you'll be welcome if you ever change your mind." Bashir smoothed it over, calming Trevino's annoyance.

Nasima understood his anger. Her Vino was still himself, and she knew better. But her next question had to be asked as well.

"What about sex?"

"We'll follow your lead and go as far as you want to go. Once again, we want to date you, Nasima. We can date without sex," Bashir replied.

She waved her hand at him. "I don't mean it like that. I mean, when we go there, I want to be enough. I want you both to be satisfied too. Will you teach me how?"

"Lil Baby, you asking me to teach you is making my dick hard, so we're already halfway there. You'll be perfect, trust me," Trevino answered.

Nasima's tongue darted out and licked her lower lip. They both stared at her, lust in their gazes. Suddenly, the room was warmer, and she wanted a demonstration. She clenched her thighs together, tried to breathe. Her nipples got hard, and she wanted hands on them.

"I don't think the three of us will have anything to worry about," Bashir whispered, finally looking away. His hand disappeared under the table, and Nasima knew he was adjusting himself. She licked her lips again, her throat dry.

"You got more questions, Lil Baby? Cause you about to be in my lap again," Trevino said.

Nasima sighed and shook her head to clear it. Focus, girl, she berated herself. You'll never get two boyfriends acting like a ninny.

"If we stay together, will y'all want to have babies with me?" she blurted out. A baby of her own was a secret dream, a long-forgotten wish she'd shoved to the back of her mind. She'd lost Trevino and didn't want anyone else for so long. Then she and Tone had so many issues she knew it'd be foolish to even contemplate tying herself to him any further. But if this worked out...would Vino and Bash give her babies?

"You're thinking of a future where we build a family? Yeah, you ours, Lil Baby. You need a minute to settle into it, but you are," Bashir said, adopting Trevino's nickname for her without a thought. Nasima liked the way he said it, liked the way it made her feel to hear it from his mouth. She smiled.

"I've been talking to Romelo about transitioning out," Trevino said, finishing his beer. Bashir got up to get him another one. "He's resistant; as far as he's concerned, we built this shit together. But this is all him. I'm a soldier, and he can get another one. When I retire, we can have all the babies you want, Nas."

"Always two steps ahead, huh, Vino?"

"I survive because I anticipate; it's all I know how to do." He shrugged. Nasima finished her wine, and Bashir poured her another glass. She stared at them, still a little shocked. These two fine ass men, one of whom she'd loved all her life, wanted to date her. Love her. Convince her to love them back. It still seemed a bit surreal.

But she couldn't deny something drew her to the two of them, to their warmth and protection. Something made her want to open her heart, her arms, and if she were being honest, her legs too. It was more than how fine they were. It was their confidence, the way they knew she belonged with them. It was their deference to her, the way they handled her so gently. And the way they anticipated her wants and needs wasn't bad, either. She took another long drink.

"Can I see the rest of the house now?" she asked. Bashir grinned. Trevino stood up.

"Come on, Lil Baby. You're gonna love the library," he said.

Twenty minutes later, she'd seen their entire house. The family room and backyard; their home gym, where Bash and Vino sparred together, and the full bathroom off to the side of it; their huge master, complete with a wall-mounted TV, en suite bathroom with walk-in closet, sitting area, and an Alaskan king-sized bed. They also showed her the other two rooms on the second floor and the bathroom connecting them—she was getting the room right next to them. Then they took her to the library/office, in their converted third-floor attic space. The house was a dream, and Nasima could see herself living in it. She didn't want to get her hopes up. This relationship dynamic test could go as badly as the first two times Vino and Bash tried. But they seemed so confident, like they knew this time would be different. Nasima could only hope they had enough confidence for her too.

"You gon date us, Lil Baby?" Trevino asked, rolling a blunt while Bashir ordered food for them. Nasima nodded. When he was relaxed and carefree like this, calling her "Lil Baby" in his sexy voice, Trevino Davis could get anything he wanted from her.

"Yes, Vino. I'll spend two weeks with you both," she confirmed. Bashir put his phone down.

"I'll get your room ready, Lil Baby. Send me a list of all your products—hair stuff, body wash and lotion, skincare, everything. I'll have it all set up by tomorrow," he said. Nasima couldn't stop her smile. They were spoiling her already.

"Okay. I'll have to keep doing my work during the day, so I need to get my laptop and a couple of other things from Smoke's house."

Trevino nodded and picked up his phone. "You want to go now?" he asked.

Nasima shook her head. She wanted a little more time away.

An hour later, she was full of lasagna and garlic bread, and they were heading back outside, this time in Bashir's forest green Range Rover. The whole ride to Smoke's house, Nasima was trying to think of the fastest way to get what she needed and leave. She didn't want there to be any fuss because if there was, Trevino would turn into Truck, and not even Candace would be safe. When they got to Smoke's three-bedroom, three-bathroom house, every light was on—including the one in her room, which was supposed to be locked. She cursed under her breath.

"How many niggas live here, anyway?" Bashir said, looking at the house with his nose scrunched up like he smelled something bad. Nasima giggled.

"My cousin Smoke, his girlfriend Candace, and Candace's little brother, Cameron. Plus, Derrick—you might know him as D-Wax—he's Smoke's cousin on his father's side, and then Tone, then me. But they're always having people over. I have my own room, and so does Cameron. Tone and D-Wax share the basement."

"Why the fuck Tone staying here?" Bashir continued with his questions.

"Because his own people know he a scammer and they don't trust him. The last aunt he stayed with got raided because he was hiding work in her basement. They don't fuck with him like that. They'll invite him to Sunday dinner and every family function, but they don't let him stay," Trevino answered, blowing smoke through his nose.

Nasima sighed. She had to get out of the car.

"I'll be five minutes, okay?" she said, opening her door. Trevino opened his too and hopped down, helping her from the backseat.

"You will. Because I'm going with you to time it," he said. Nasima opened her mouth to argue, saw the look on his face, and knew there was no use.

"If it helps, I took his gun. Long as they don't fuck with you, shouldn't be no issues, Lil Baby," Bashir said, leaning back against the seat with the blunt Trevino passed him when he got out of the car.

Nasima grabbed Vino's hand and went to the door. She used her key and opened it, pulling him into the living room with her. Everyone was home, and three of Smoke's friends were also there. Nasima knew he was pissed she hadn't been there to make dinner.

"Fuck you been all day?" Smoke demanded, not even looking up.

"With me," Trevino said quietly, and everyone in the room stopped moving. Smoke looked up, his eyes widening. Nasima understood. Some people saw Truck Davis and it was the last thing they ever saw. Tone looked like he might shit himself, and Nasima took great delight in his fear.

"I'm gonna go hang out with Vino for a few days. I came to get some stuff," she said, moving toward the stairs.

"I-I'm still expecting your rent, Nas," Smoke called after her, stuttering a little.

"If your own blood paying rent, I know these niggas better be paying some too," Trevino said, pointing to Tone, Candace, and her brother. Candace looked like she might say something, but her brother shook his head. Smoke pretended to laugh.

"I-I don't tell you how to run your house, Truck," he said, trying to stand up for himself.

Trevino laughed—a dark, dangerous laugh—and everyone in the room wondered if they would survive the night. "You right, my nigga. I'm looking out for Nas. I'd hate to find out somebody was taking advantage of her, you know? That's my heart. Get your stuff, Lil Baby. I'll be right here waiting."

Nasima ran upstairs and into her room. It looked like someone had been in her bed and rifling through her drawers. She grabbed her laptop, a folder of important work papers, and some of her clothes, underwear, and books. She threw everything into a duffle and went to the closet, pushing back a floor panel in the back and removing her box of private information. Then she grabbed the duffle, her two broken locks, and the box and went back downstairs. She dropped the broken locks in her cousin's lap.

"Someone broke into my room," she said and turned away, handing Trevino her box and duffle bag. "I'm ready."

"I'm not, though. Somebody was in your shit? This the first time it happened?" Trevino demanded.

"Yes, but I'm not usually gone for so long," Nasima said, nodding.

"Don't matter, Nas. Nigga charging you rent, you a tenant. You supposed to have an expectation of privacy in this bitch. Smoke, I usually let you make it cause you her cousin, but you about to make me turn into somebody you don't want to meet."

"Truck, wait—"

"Vino, don't—"

"Truth be told, I owe you a bullet just off the strength of the way you came at her when she walked in here. Nas, anything else up there you want, get it now. You done here," Trevino said, cutting them both off.

No one else in the room said anything or even moved. Candace looked like she wanted to cry. Nasima shook her head. She had everything important to her. Now she needed to get Vino out of here before he killed her cousin.

He turned back to Smoke, a deep frown on his face. Before anyone could blink, he smashed his fist into Smoke's face, knocking him off his chair and onto the floor. Nasima gasped, Smoke howled in pain, and everyone else sat there, shocked into silence. Tone stood up, backing away on shaking legs and escaping into the kitchen. The back door slammed moments later.

"I have everything I want. Let's go," Nas said, trying to pull Trevino away.

"Nas is your blood. You charging her rent and letting these freeloading ass niggas steal from her?" he asked him. Smoke shook his head, holding his face and moaning in pain.

"Nah, I wouldn't— I didn't know about nobody going in your room, Nas," Smoke rushed to explain, his words muffled and broken. Trevino stepped forward, glaring like he didn't believe him. Nasima put her hand on Trevino's back, calming him. She wasn't too concerned about her cousin, but she was concerned about Vino expending his energy on a place she was never coming back to.

"Vino, I want to go," she insisted. He turned to her, dialing his anger back as soon as he saw her body language. He nodded and turned back to face the room.

"A'ight, Nas. Smoke, you know who I am, so you know I'm a see you," Trevino said, pointing at Smoke, then looking toward the kitchen where Tone had run away. "You and Tone."

Nasima walked out the door and he followed, but not before giving them one more maniacal laugh. When they got to the Range Rover, Bashir was singing along with his playlist. He took one look at Trevino's face and sat up straight in the seat.

"What happened?" he asked. Trevino made sure Nasima was in the car, then got in too, scowling.

"She had locks on her door, and he let them break in. You know that nigga charging her rent? I know she the only one paying it too. Nas, you not giving him another fucking dime, you hear me? If I had my own car, I'd have got the grenade launcher from the trunk and leveled the whole fucking house. Matta fact, Butta, give me my gun."

"Vino!" Nasima protested, trying to make him calm down. He shook his head.

"Nah, fuck that—"

"Let's get Nas home, Trev. You see how upset she is," Bashir reasoned. Trevino took a deep breath, trying to regulate himself.

"I meant what I said. Whether you want us or not, staying there is dead. Do you understand me, Nasima Amara?" he said, using her full name to show her he wasn't playing.

"Yes, Trevino," she said. He only used her full name when he was worried for her or needed her to do what he said without question. And she heeded his words. He'd never steered her wrong before.

Once they were back at the house, Nasima suggested they watch movies together, and Trevino and Bashir agreed, even going so far as to pop popcorn and offer her candy. They watched two movies before she felt herself drifting off. She lay on her side between them, her head in Trevino's lap and her feet in Bashir's. Occasionally, she'd look up to see them smiling at each other, or holding hands across the top of the couch. Nasima liked watching them. Their love was so obvious, so real. Offering her a space in their lives felt like a dream to Nasima, and an unrealistic wish. But Vino never lied to her. If he said there was room for her, she'd trust him and try her hardest to believe there was.

Chapter 3

Nasima

Three Days Later

Nasima yawned, opening her eyes and stretching her arms out wide. She was in the queen-sized bed in the guest room next to Bash and Vino's master. She sat up, stretching her body more, pulling her tank top down over her belly. Her fatness pushed out anyway, the same way her thighs devoured the lounging shorts she was wearing. Waking up in this house gave her such a warm feeling. Nasima was excited to see her guys; she'd missed them all night.

The last three days had been a satisfying glimpse into the life of Vino and Bash. After getting her things, they'd taken her home and watched movies with her until she fell asleep. And the next day, no one woke her. Nasima woke on her own at eleven a.m. No one yelled for breakfast, no one objectified her body, no one gave her attitude for not waking earlier. They let her be and fed her when she got up like it was okay for her to sleep until nearly lunchtime.

She logged into work and finished her assignments, and then the shopping started. Vino and Bash took Nasima to the mall and bought her a full wardrobe, from leggings and shirts, sweats, and cargos to underwear and sleep clothes. She got a new coat and boots, and her old ones went right into the trash at the mall. They didn't miss a step. They even got her hair and nails done.

Then the three of them went back to the house, where a man pulling a trailer met them. Nasima found out the trailer was full of sneakers, the latest styles and the most valuable retros, in every colorway she could imagine. Bash took great pleasure in choosing her footwear, saying she had to be as fly as they were. Whenever she protested, Vino told her he would spend his money where he pleased, and her only job was to take advantage of it. The closet in her bedroom was bursting at the seams now, but Bash simply shrugged and said,

"We'll find a way to extend it if we have to. Or you can come sleep with us, and the entire bedroom can become your closet."

Nasima didn't have a response. Sleeping with them intrigued her; she'd love to settle into being more intimate with them, but she couldn't help feeling like an interruption or a distraction. Bash and Vino had a rhythm to them, a cadence. They were in sync, so much so she loved simply watching them. The last thing she wanted to be was a disruption.

But they made everything so easy to get used to. They cooked her dinner and took her to a drive-in movie after spending an obscene amount of money on her sneakers. Then they all stayed up talking by the fire pit in the backyard, Bash and Vino telling her about their relationship while they passed a blunt back and forth.

The next day, Bashir went to check on his gym, and she and Trevino had a chance to spill out all their emotions about the time they'd spent apart. It was cleansing, and after talking themselves to tears, the two of them shared their first real kiss in years. Vino's lips were hard on hers, urgent. He lapped her up with his thick tongue, exploring her until she whimpered and clung to him. When they broke apart, she was damp in her panties, and her nipples stood at attention, but she didn't have the nerve to tell him to go further. She didn't know if Bashir would feel a way about her not waiting until they were all together. Vino grabbed her ass in his hands and brought her against his hard dick.

"When it's Butta's turn, he'll be here, Lil Baby. This moment is about you and me. Don't overthink it. We don't need nobody's permission but ours to kiss and touch, and we're not leaving anyone out."

After his assurance, she felt better, so they kissed some more, and she was able to rub his head and suck on his neck while he growled under her touch. Vino sucked her nipples and reached into her sleep shorts with his large fingers, rubbing her swollen clit until she came, calling his name. Nasima hadn't been touched so good in years.

When Bashir came home, he had a giant bouquet of flowers for her and a bag of smokable flower for Trevino. Then he and Vino went into the gym to spar, and she watched, loving the way their bodies danced around each other. The two of them grunted and mumbled things to each other, their sweat dotting their bodies, their intimacy unmatched. The intricate way they threw and blocked punches, encouraged and praised each other, pushed each other further, was a sensual dance, a rhythm specific to them. Nasima got wet watching them, her mind playing pictures of her swallowing one of them with her mouth and the other with her pussy at the same time. She could barely breathe she was so aroused, and her hands shook with the need to interrupt their training and touch them.

After training, Nasima went to her room to work, needing to get her body under control. The second day ended with a dinner date at a fancy restaurant. Bash and Vino took turns feeding her, and as she greedily sucked food off their fingers, she'd never felt so cherished and so seduced at the same time.

Back home, they cuddled with her between them on the huge sectional, kissing her face, lips, and neck. Nasima kissed them both back, feeling out of control and lustful, but still so loved. She fell asleep between them. And now, she was in her own bed, her body pulsing with the need to be touched, and Nasima knew today she would tell them so.

She got up, brushed her teeth, washed her face, then put a thin robe over her sleep set and headed downstairs. When she got to the bottom, she heard Bash moaning and stopped just short of being seen.

She peered around the wall and into the kitchen. Bash and Vino were kissing passionately, Vino's strong hands wrapped around Bashir's thick dick. He pumped as they kissed, running his thumb over the mushroom head. Bash moaned louder, his arms around Vino's neck. Their lips pressed together as their tongues thrashed, and Nasima was suddenly so wet it was almost running down her legs. She'd never seen them so...uninhibited.

"You gon wake Lil Baby," Vino cautioned between kisses. Bash pulled away smiling, biting his lip as Trevino continued to massage his dick.

"I can't wait to see her underneath you, babe," he said, lowering his voice. Nasima's hands went to her breasts, and she squeezed her nipples, the stimulation making her shake. Trevino laughed—the dark, menacing laugh she loved—and jerked Bashir's dick harder.

"Yeah? I can't wait for you to ride my dick while she rides my face."

"She's gonna stay, right, Trev? I want her so badly, and I know you need her. She's ours, Trev. Nobody else can have her—"

"Shhh, Butta," Trevino said, leaning to kiss his lover again. "Calm down, baby. I know Nas. She needs a little time, but she'll remember herself soon. Remember her power. Then she'll open her heart. I know it."

Nasima felt her heart in her throat. They needed her and wanted her to belong to them. It was enough to set off her nerves, even as it aroused her body.

"I love you, Trevino," Bashir said, unwrapping his arms from around Trevino's neck and dropping to his knees. He pulled on Vino's sweatpants and his long, thick dick popped out, bobbing up and down, hard and ready. Bashir licked the vein on the underside from nuts to tip and then sucked the head into his mouth, his eyes fluttering closed.

"Gotdamn, Butta. I love you too," Trevino bit out, bracing himself on the island. He moved his hips, fucking Bashir's mouth, moaning as he looked down at his lover. Nasima whimpered, rubbing her nipples harder. Her clit swelled and her pussy lips quivered. Bashir sucked faster, took more of Vino's length, moaning as he slurped. He worked Vino's long, fat dick in and out of his mouth with the erotic precision of someone who knew his body and heart. Trevino threw his head back and closed his eyes, moving one hand to the back of Bashir's head. Bash squeezed Vino's balls, sucked harder, worked his jaws. He opened his eyes again and stared up at his lover, taking him to the brink of orgasm with love in his eyes.

"Fuck, I'm 'bout to nut," Trevino managed to moan, still thrusting his hips, lost in the pleasure of Bashir's warm mouth. Nasima could feel herself moving toward the edge, and she was dying to touch herself. She backed up the stairway as quietly as she could and heard Trevino yell his release as she shut her room door. Her pussy contracted and she dropped to her knees, coming hard as her mind filled with a replay of the things she'd seen—the length and thickness of hard dicks, their strong hands and wet mouths. Nasima whimpered and shook. Her orgasm stole her breath as her chest heaved, and she clapped her hands over her mouth, not wanting to be found out.

A moment later, the sensations subsided, and she was finally able to move to the bed. She sat down on the edge, regaining her breath. Nasima licked her lips, feeling like she needed water. A few minutes later, there was a knock on her room door.

"Lil Baby? We're checking on you. You okay?"

"Nas, you've been sleeping a long time. Come eat, baby love," Bashir followed.

"Come in, please," she called to them.

The door opened and the two of them walked in, looking relaxed and in love. They sat on either side of her.

"What's wrong, Lil Baby? What happened?" Trevino demanded.

"You're all flushed, Nas. Are you feeling sick?" Bashir said, pressing the back of his hand to her forehead and neck.

Nasima looked up at them and bit her lip. It was now or never.

"I want to make love. I want you to make me come."

Bashir

As soon as Nasima's words registered in his brain, Bashir blinked. Then he blinked again. His dick woke from its short slumber and his hands got warm. Nas was ready for them.

He looked up at Trevino and caught his grin. Trev had told him she would come around. And Bashir desired her so much he could barely stand it. Watching her walk around the house was both a slow torture and a special kind of joy. He was so happy they'd filled her closet with clothing that clung to her and displayed all her jiggle and bounce, showing off her softness. She was damn near naked now, wearing a skimpy sleep set and telling them to make her come. It was a dream come true.

He leaned down and kissed her, taking her by surprise and stealing her mouth. He swallowed her gasp as he tasted her, sliding his tongue between her lips and pressing his lips against hers. Nasima kissed him back, her hands coming up to comb through his beard. Bashir groaned, loving her touch, and promised himself the beard she loved so much would be soaked in her juice before the day was done.

Trevino buried his face in Nas's neck, kissing her there as he plucked her hard nipples. Nasima whimpered into his mouth and tangled her tongue with his, pushing her titties into Trevino's hands. Bashir inhaled, then sucked at her lips, certain the taste of her could sustain him for the rest of his life.

"Let's go," Trev ordered, lifting his head. "We belong in our bed." He stood up and grabbed their hands, pulling them behind him. Once they were next door in the master, he let their hands go, pushing down his sweatpants and stepping out of them. His impressive dick was waking up, stretching and thickening.

Bashir licked his lips as he pushed his own sweats off and pulled his t-shirt over his head. He sat down on the bed, pulling Nasima between his legs. Trev got into bed too, getting on his knees behind him and massaging his shoulders. Bash moaned. Trev's hands were the perfect combination of roughness and finesse. He looked up at Nas, standing in front of him, shaking like a leaf. But he knew her quivering body was filled with desire, not fear; he could see it in her eyes. Bashir tugged at her shirt, getting it off her. Her titties bounced near his mouth, and he caught one, licking around the nipple and suckling her.

"Ohhhhh," Nasima breathed, her hands going to his shoulders. He tasted her breast, his fingers pulling and tugging the nipple he wasn't sucking. Soft cries pushed from her mouth, and she shook even more. Trevino kissed and sucked on his neck, bit his shoulders, rubbed his back. Bashir knew he was as aroused as Nasima, and it made his heart pound. He was responsible for making them want like this. He held the keys to their desire. They were his, and no one else's.

He switched to Nasima's other nipple while he pulled down her shorts and moved a hand down between her thighs. The entrance to her pussy was so wet, her slickness creamy and thick like she'd been coming already.

"You come in your sleep, Lil Baby?" he asked, releasing her nipple momentarily. "You been dreaming about us?" He slid his thumb over her clit and heard her breath hitch as he started to play in her pussy.

"I wasn't dreaming," she whispered, widening her stance to give him more access. "I was watching. I saw—the kitchen—"

"You saw us pleasing each other, Nas? That's what got you all worked up like this?" Trevino asked. She nodded, and her two men smiled at each other. Bashir stopped his touching.

"Get on the bed, baby," he instructed.

Nasima climbed into bed, situating herself in the middle on the mountain of pillows. Bashir lay on one side of her, Trevino on the other. Trev gripped her by the throat, not enough to hurt or frighten but enough to get her attention.

"Why you ain't come join us, Lil Baby? These dicks yours as much as they ours. I could have put you on the island and gobbled that pussy like Butta was gobbling my dick."

"I was nervous. I didn't— Vino, I need you. Both of you," Nasima answered, spreading her thighs.

Bashir chuckled and went back to playing in her pussy. Her breath caught as his fingers went inside her. He plunged them in and out, hearing her creaminess and feeling the grip of her pussy. Trevino had taken over sucking her nipples and now Nasima was moaning loudly, head thrashing back and forth, her body tightening as she got ready to come.

"Yes—oh, fuck—yes, oh yes," she babbled, her essence sliding down his fingers and into his palm. Bashir was so hard it hurt, in awe of this gorgeous, passionate creature next to him. Trevino kissed her mouth, rubbed her breasts, and pulled on her nipples. A second later, Nasima's back arched, her pussy squirted, and she belted out a strangled scream. She shook violently as her orgasm crashed over her, her tight pussy contracting around his fingers.

"Baaaaaash," she wailed, and Bashir had never heard a sexier sound in his life. He pressed on her clit, prolonging the pleasure, and watched her hips move as she came again. Both he and Trevino were in her ear, telling her how sexy she was, how they loved seeing her come, how they couldn't wait to do it again.

When Nasima was calm again, she turned to Trevino, kissing him passionately. Then they stared at each other, communicating something with their eyes. She nodded and turned back to him, grabbing his dick in her hand.

"I want to ride you until I come again."

Bashir smirked. "You got moves, Lil Baby?" he challenged her.

"Vino taught me," she said with a smile, and he laughed from the other side of the bed. She pushed Bashir on his back, and he elevated his upper half with pillows. Nasima licked the head of his dick and sucked it into her mouth, moaning as she suctioned her jaws. Bashir cursed; her mouth was lethal.

"Nas, what the fuck?" he asked as she sucked him to his hardest. She massaged his balls and took his thickness into her throat, her head bobbing up and down. She poked her ass out, and Trevino slid two fingers into her pussy from behind. Nasima whimpered, moving her hips, sucking him into oblivion. Bashir grabbed a handful of her hair, rubbed her scalp, and wondered if he was losing his mind.

When Nasima sat up, Trev pulled his fingers away. She straddled Bashir, lining up his thick head with her wet opening. She sank down on his dick, crying out as she took inch after inch of him. When he was fully inside, Bashir smacked her ass, and they both moaned. Her pussy was ocean wet with a vice grip. He was lost. This woman could have everything he owned, and all his heart too.

"Bash..." She called his name and began to move, bracing her hands on his chest so she could slide up and down on his dick. She got into a rhythm, cursing and closing her eyes. Bashir moaned, knowing he'd never doubt her again. Her hips danced and swayed as she fucked them both into the mattress.

Bashir looked over, and Trevino was jerking himself off, watching them. Damn, he thought. He had a fine ass nigga with a big dick, and he had the best pussy in the world wrapped around him. What a life.

"Ride this dick, Lil Baby," he encouraged, "give me my pussy."

"I'm coming. I'm coming again, Bashir!" Nasima yelled out and kept riding, clenching his dick as her pussy began to contract. He saw her cream sliding down his dick as she raised and lowered herself. Bashir reached up and tugged on her nipples. Nasima screamed, taking his dick to the balls, digging her nails into his chest. She closed her eyes; her body jerked. Her pussy gripped him over and over as she came and came.

"Fuck!" Bashir yelled, coming too. His nut shot out of him, coating her walls. His toes curled and his eyes crossed. In the distance, he heard Trev moan. Nasima fell forward onto him, and Bashir kissed her forehead. Trevino got up, going into the bathroom.

"Told you I had moves," Nas said, still catching her breath. Bashir laughed.

"I'll never doubt you again," he promised, rubbing her back. Trevino came back into the room, carrying wet rags and a towel.

"Y'all mufuckas better than porn," he said, shaking his head. Bashir and Nasima laughed. Nas sat up, getting off him. She let Trevino wipe her down and put her in his t-shirt. Then he wiped Bashir down, kissing him gently.

"She wore your ass out, didn't she?" he asked. Bashir smirked.

"You knew she would," he said back. Trev nodded.

"I taught her," he said, winking.

Trevino

Watching Butta and Lil Baby make love shifted something inside of Trevino; it felt like he was falling deeper, harder, and with more intention than ever. These two were his entire life, the owners of his heart and dick and every other piece of him. His fine ass nigga and his gorgeous fat mama—his world revolved around them now and always would. They were the reason. He held Nasima tight to his body, rubbing her and kissing her forehead. Bashir came to them, snuggling close and throwing a blanket over all three of them.

"We can't go to sleep," Trevino said, yawning. "Lil Baby hasn't eaten anything yet today."

"I want you to hold me, Vino," Nasima said, sounding drowsy. "Please don't let me go."

"Never again, Nas. I'll never let you go again," he promised. He kissed her forehead again, then found Butta's lips, kissing him too.

"Rest, Trev. I'll feed everyone when we wake up. Rest," Bashir insisted. Trevino nodded and pulled his family close, finally closing his eyes.

He awoke first, an hour and a half later, and found himself trapped. Nasima was sprawled on top of him, arms wrapped around his middle, while Bashir had drifted downward and was on his legs, his head on Trevino's thighs. He laughed softly. We got this big ass bed so we could sleep in a ball every night, he thought. But he wouldn't have it any other way.

He shifted Nasima over, kissing her hair and trying to settle her back down. She whimpered in protest, reaching for him. Trevino grinned. He tried rubbing Bashir's head and moving him gently, but Butta pushed his hands away and settled against his legs again.

"Okay," Trevino said, sighing. "I was trying to do this without waking y'all, but I gotta pee. Butta, Lil Baby, come on and get up. The two of you are literally on top of me," he said, nudging them. Nasima opened her eyes and smiled at him.

"You're warm, Vino," she whispered. Trevino laughed and kissed her softly. Bashir opened his eyes next, realizing where he was. He rolled over, and Trevino finally stretched his legs.

"Sorry, babe," Butta said, moving back up on the bed. He lay behind Nasima and pulled her back into his front, burying his face in her neck and closing his eyes again. Nasima settled down again as well, and Trevino shook his head, getting out of bed.

He used the bathroom and took a quick shower, slathering his body with lotion and putting on a clean t-shirt and boxers. He left his loves sleeping soundly and went down to the kitchen to see what he could put together for them. Seeing they were mostly stocked up with breakfast items, he made bacon, sausage, and French toast, leaving them in the oven to warm while he woke Butta and Lil Baby. They were both still snuggled together. Trevino smiled. He was getting more domestic by the hour. The sheer pleasure he was taking from watching his family come together was unlike anything he'd ever felt. It made him think about the past.

Sending Nas away was a necessary step for both of them. She'd deserved a life away from the man he was while he was building things with Romelo. And she'd deserved a life away from a place where no one had her back except him, not even her bitch ass cousin. He'd always hoped she was off making friends, taking vacations, going to brunch and happy hour with her coworkers and living her life. Knowing Tone conspired to fuck it up for her made him angry. But a small part of him felt like he couldn't be too mad at life bringing her back into his arms. Bashir told him if he had one more dream about her, they were going to get her. He saw her at the Diner the next day. Maybe they were inevitable after all.

He sat down on the bed and leaned over, kissing Nasima's luscious mouth until she woke up and kissed him back. When her beautiful whiskey eyes were open, he repeated the kisses with Bashir.

"Mmm, Trev, you taste good," Butta said, licking his lips and opening his eyes. Trevino looked down at them, his heart speeding up.

"You and Lil Baby need to come downstairs. I didn't want to make the eggs until y'all were up," he said. Nasima sat up, pushing hair out of her face.

"I'm up, Vino. I'm hungry too. And I need to log in and see if I have any work to do today."

"While you on the computer, you need to start looking for a job you like. Because I know you're bored with the bullshit you're doing now. I been meaning to make you quit," Trevino said, frowning. Nasima rolled her eyes and got out of bed, escaping to the bathroom.

"Don't press her so hard, Trev," Butta said, turning onto his back. "Nas needs to keep her independence, you know that. Let her have this. We can upgrade around it. She'll realize she don't need it no more in her own time."

"Fine, Butta, I'll back off. But she should know I ain't about to watch her struggle—"

"She knows, Trev. But we sprung a lot on her in a few days. The job is something familiar, and I think we should let her keep it," Bashir continued.

Trevino sighed. Not being able to lift a burden from his Lil Baby was fucking with his head. He didn't know how to stop providing and protecting where she was concerned. Nobody brought it out of him quite like she did. He rolled his shoulders and stood up. Butta got up too and pulled him close, kissing him. Trevino fell into his love, into the softness of his kiss, and felt his angst settle. Their tongues wrapped around each other, and Butta moaned. Trevino grabbed his ass, and their bodies ground against each other.

"Stop worrying," Butta said with one last juicy kiss. "She's fine. She's here with us, she's safe and happy. And if your slick ass mouth does what it's supposed to, she'll stay."

Trevino cracked up, holding Bashir to him for a moment more before letting him go. The two of them heard the shower come on in their bathroom. They looked at each other.

"I know you want her coming in your beard. Don't take too long; I'm starting the eggs," Trevino said, smirking. Bashir smiled and bit his lip, then headed to Nasima in the bathroom.

Bashir and Nasima came down thirty minutes later, Nasima dressed in Butta's t-shirt and a pair of leggings, her feet covered in socks. Her eyes were glazed with lust, low and satisfied. Butta was grinning, wearing a pair of sweatshorts and a tank top. She walked up to Trevino and wrapped her arms around him.

"Missed you in the shower," she said low, taking a seat at the table. He smiled and started making plates. Bashir poured orange juice for himself, iced coffee for Nasima, and hot coffee for Trevino, and they all sat down to eat. For long moments, there was nothing but the sound of chewing. Trevino looked around, still in awe at how his life had settled so much in a few days.

"No matter how hard I try, I can't get my scrambled eggs like this, Trev," Butta said around a mouthful of food.

"I know, right? He's had this egg magic since we were kids. He used to feed me a lot—my parents didn't really remember they had a daughter most of the time—and I loved his scrambled eggs. I can eat breakfast all day if Vino is making it," Nasima agreed.

Trevino grinned. He didn't mind them gassing him because he knew they meant it. "I'm glad y'all like it. But y'all took longer than I thought to come downstairs, so now we're out of bananas—and blackberries."

"Dammit, Trev, I was gonna put those bananas in a smoothie," Butta protested, shaking his head. Trevino shrugged. Nasima giggled.

When their plates were clean, they went to the couch. Nas checked in on her laptop and did some work, and he and Butta watched TV. After her work was done, Nasima snuggled next to him, rubbing his chest as she stared at the television. She hummed a song under her breath, like she was soothing him. Her delicate scent wafted up from her body, mixed with lingering notes of Butta because she was wearing his shirt. Trevino couldn't help it; his dick got hard. He nudged her face up to his and kissed her, sucking on her lips and slipping his tongue into her mouth. Nasima moaned, pressed closer, and moved her mouth against his.

They kissed for long moments, tasting and rediscovering each other. The love of their past swirled around them, mixed with this new love, sitting on their old foundation and building something different. Trevino loved the way her body felt against his, the way her mouth felt against his. He couldn't believe he'd gone without it for so long. He pushed Nasima back until she was lying on the sectional, settling on top of her. He released her mouth and lifted her shirt, latching onto her nipple and licking.

"Vino—" Her moan of his name was muffled by Butta covering her mouth with his. Trevino smiled and kept suckling, rubbing her other nipple between his fingers. He kissed her stomach, imagining it full of him and Butta's babies as he moved to her other breast. He licked and kissed her nipples while she writhed underneath him and Butta kissed her soft mouth. Trevino leaned up and dragged her leggings and underwear off, getting annoyed at the extra barrier.

"No panties in my fucking house," he growled. Nasima whimpered and spread her thighs, already ready for him.

"Do you hear me, Nasima Amara?" he said, tossing her clothes to the floor and pushing two fingers into her soaked pussy.

"Yes, Vino. I-I won't do it again," she said, lifting her hips to take more of his fingers. She cried out softly, begging to be filled. Trevino rubbed her clit with his thumb while he worked his hand inside her. Nasima wailed, her pussy tightening around his fingers. She came in a flash, her moans going into Butta's mouth because he hadn't stopped kissing her.

Trevino pulled his fingers from her body, putting them in his mouth and sucking her cream off them. He stood up, pulling off his tank and pushing his sweatpants down. Kicking out of them, he kneeled on the couch. He grabbed his dick, rubbing it as he stared at his woman and her pretty pussy. Nasima was biting her lower lip, those whiskey eyes closed, waiting for him to fill her. He leaned in, put his dick at the entrance to her pussy, and pressed forward. He heard Lil Baby's sharp intake of breath, heard Butta curse as he watched. But all he could feel was warm wetness, tight and familiar. Nasima fit him like a glove; she always had. Trevino moaned, unable to help himself.

"Welcome home, Vino," Nasima whispered, and her words turned him into a savage, intent on claiming her the way he once had. He thrust hard, pushing her thighs open and burying himself to the balls. Nas reached for him, called his name. Butta played with her titties, increasing her stimulation, making her run even wetter around him. Trevino pulled out and thrust in again, then again, needing to feel her, take her.

"Why you give Tone my pussy, Nas? Huh? You knew that nigga wasn't worthy," he bit out, fucking her fiercely. Lil Baby opened her eyes, shook her head, tried to regain her breath.

"Vino, I was lonely. I was so l-lonely," she stuttered out. He kept fucking her, shaking his head.

"You should have come to me before you gave my pussy away."

"He showed me—he showed me you and Bash. You looked so happy, baby. You looked happy. I didn't want— and then he was there. He kept coming around. Vino, I—"

"Tell me you didn't love him," Trevino demanded, out of his mind with jealousy and anger. Tone wasn't even good enough to sniff her, let alone put his dick inside. Lil Baby had no business sharing her treasure with a snake like him. She should have come to him, so he could take care of her.

"Vino, I've only ever loved you," she moaned, rolling into an orgasm. Her body shook; her pussy clenched. She choked his dick as she came and came, tears running down her cheeks. Butta soothed her, whispering in her ear, keeping her from getting overstimulated. Trevino slowed down his thrusts, pushing himself firmly inside over and over. The room was spinning. Her pussy was magic. He could feel everything around him. He was going over the edge, falling deep in her ocean where he would gladly drown.

"Thank you for coming home, Lil Baby," he said, grabbing her hands. Trevino closed his eyes and groaned as his orgasm swept over him, making his nut shoot out and his toes curl. Nasima whined, dug her nails into his skin, and came all over again. Trevino fell on top of her, kissing her lips.

"Thank you for being my home, Vino," his Lil Baby whispered in his ear, and Trevino knew there was no turning back.

Chapter 4

Nasima

Nasima fully embraced being a big girl, and a pretty one. Tone had done a number on her self-confidence, but she never forgot how good she looked and felt when she dressed up, when she was happy enough to let her personality show through. She was aware she was finer than most, extra pounds or not. And her extra pounds only made folks want to grab and rub, even when it was her jiggly arms, her belly, or her back fat. Vino and Bash called her their gorgeous fat mama, and she welcomed their appreciation and lust. But even with her own certainties and their reassurance, Nasima still found herself nervous when it was time to ride faces. An entire shelf of belly, her ham hock thighs, and a dump truck ass wouldn't let her feel a hundred percent calm about blocking someone's airway. But when the someone was Bashir Rosewood, thinking you weren't going to give him what he wanted was a fool's game.

And so here she was, her hips moving back and forth, her mouth open in ecstasy, strangled cries coming from her throat as she rode this man's face and dripped the pleasure he created right onto his beard. Bashir's tongue was a weapon, drawing out her will, making her weak, attacking her defenses. Nasima trembled, on the verge of coming for the second time. The lower half of Bashir's face was sticky and wet from her first orgasm, and Nasima's eyes rolled back, the sweet sensations of him sucking on her clit like peppermint candy nearly too much to bear.

Below, Bashir was thrusting his hips upward as his thick dick was sucked into Trevino's mouth. Nasima's nipples were so hard they hurt; her body was on fire. Feeling the pleasure Bashir was giving and watching the pleasure he was taking made her wetter than she could ever remember being.

How did the sex keep getting better? More intense? Their connection was the only answer, and it was growing so fast. Trevino moaned, slurped, and gobbled Bashir's dick like it was the best thing he'd ever tasted, and Nasima wanted to come right then. She loved seeing him this way, at the mercy of a lover who was at the mercy of his mouth. And it was one talented ass mouth. Vino cupped his balls and massaged them. Bashir grunted, and his tongue swirled over her pussy lips, catching her passionate drippings. Nasima shook, bounced her hips, and tried to get away, but Bashir slapped her on the ass and held her still, taking her breath with his tongue and lips.

"Baaaaaash!" she screamed, feeling her pussy gushing, the muscles tightening and relaxing as her orgasm spun her away. Nasima pulled on her own nipples as she rode his face, prolonging the pleasure. Bashir licked up all her cream, moaning as Trevino picked up speed. Trevino growled and took Bashir's dick fully until he was gagging. Nasima managed to lift herself slightly, trying to move finally, and Bashir cried out, his hips jerking upward.

"Trev! Yes, baby," he yelled, shutting his eyes and releasing his nut. Trevino swallowed it all, still sucking on him, not letting up. Nasima moved down next to Bashir and kissed his nipples, running her tongue around them, wanting to prolong his pleasure too.

"Shit... I can't— Fuck, oh yes," he babbled, shaking a little himself. Trevino finally released his dick and sat up, licking his lips. He kissed Bashir's thigh, then his stomach.

"You good, Butta?" he asked, coming up to the other side of him. He reached for Nasima's hand, and she gave it to him. They lay watching their sweet baby Bashir come down from his amazing orgasm.

"Y'all two..." Bashir said while pointing at them, his light brown face flushed, his beard wet and shiny. "Between your sweet ass pussy and your slick ass mouth, I'm worn out."

"Y'all got me spoiled," Nasima said, laughing. "I came into this bed three nights ago and nobody can keep their hands, mouths, or dicks to themselves. It's not my fault."

"You fine as fuck, that pussy fire, and your mouth should be outlawed. Take some responsibility," Trevino said, laughing too.

Bashir smiled as he looked at them. The love and satisfaction in his gaze still scared Nasima a bit, but she was liking it more and more by the day. And liking him more and more. After a week with Vino and Bash, she was certain she'd stay. Living in this house was a dream come true. She never did any more or less than exactly what she wanted. And they hadn't attempted to domesticate her in any way. Vino and Bash never asked her to cook, clean, do laundry, or organize their lives. They never tried to coerce or guilt her into their bed, nor did they ever ask her for anything in return for what they gave her. And while part of her expected this— because it was Vino and he loved her—she hadn't been sure how the dynamic of two men might change things. But if anything, Bashir was almost more solicitous than Trevino. Vino said it was because he was trying to impress her.

Nasima was impressed. And she wanted both men—in her life, in her bed, and in her pussy for the rest of her days. But maybe it was too soon to tell them. Valentine's Day was still a week away.

"I'm weak as fuck. I'm supposed to go check on the gym today," Bashir said. Trevino nodded.

"Get yo ass up, then. But for real, me and Lil Baby will come with you. She hasn't been to the boxing gym since before you owned it, and I want her to see how you've upgraded. We can get something to eat too," he said. He stretched his arms out and made himself get out of bed, holding out his hands for theirs. Nasima gave Trevino her hand, and he pulled her from the sheets, holding her close and kissing her forehead. Bashir took his other hand, and Trevino hauled him up too.

"We sweated out your hair, Lil Baby. I'm a take you to get it done again tomorrow, okay?" Vino said. Nasima's first instinct was to protest, say she would manage, tell him not to waste his money. But this past week was teaching her, slowly but surely, that Vino and Bash *needed* to care for her. They wanted her to know she was covered and protected. They wanted her to know her needs and wants would be fulfilled. And sometimes, she had to step back and let them. She thought of it as spoiling, but for them, it was simply a requirement of being her men. So she nodded, like the obedient baby she was.

"Okay," she said back. Vino hit her with one of his dazzling smiles, and she knew he was happy she hadn't put up a fight. She turned out of his arms and headed for her room next door.

"Nas, where you going?" Bash asked her, his brows wrinkled in confusion. She smiled.

"My clothes are next door, so it's easier for me to shower there. Plus, as spacious as your bathroom is, it's not really made for *three* people. Fat Mama needs her space," she replied, pointing to herself and laughing. Vino frowned.

"We can make space for you, Nas," he said, sounding angry.

Nasima shook her head. "You already did—you gave me *my own bathroom.* And it's perfect. I'll meet y'all right back here in thirty minutes or so."

"Lil Baby, I don't want you to think—"

"I don't think it, baby. I'm fine. And I hate when you're upset, my love, so please don't be upset," she said, coming back to hug Vino around his middle. He sighed, like he was disappointed in himself, but he rubbed her back and let it be. Bashir bent down and kissed her lips. Nasima smiled, letting Vino go and heading to get dressed.

She came back into the room forty-five minutes later, dressed in ripped dark wash jeans, a cropped pink sweater, and a pair of hot pink 270s, her hair tamed in a ponytail with her edges slicked down. Bashir was already dressed in olive green chinos, a white button-down shirt, and a pair of dark brown chukkas. He was fastening a watch on his wrist.

"You look good, baby," Nasima said, unable to help herself. She caught the scent of him in her nose and her body reacted. Bash grinned.

"I'm only here to keep up with you, love. You look edible right now."

"Thank you," she said, smiling shyly. "Where's Vino?"

"In the bathroom, trying to figure out how to extend it so it's big enough for the three of us," Bashir said, shaking his head. Nasima sighed.

"Trevino Davis, you get out of there! I said it was fine!" she yelled.

Vino came out of the bathroom, looking sexy as hell in denim-colored joggers, a long-sleeved red t-shirt, and red, white, and blue 1s on his feet. There was a deep frown on his face, but it only made him sexier to Nasima.

"You should be in here with us," he insisted. Nasima rolled her eyes. Stubborn man.

"Trev, how about we extend the hall bathroom, turn it into a spa especially for Nas?" Bashir tried to compromise. Nasima shook her head.

"The bathroom is fine the way it is—both of them," she said.

Trevino shook his head. He reached out, grabbed her sweater, and yanked her into his arms. Nasima yelped in surprise.

"You belong with us," he said, his voice low and urgent. "The two of us already lost each other once. I sent you away instead of figuring out how to give you what you needed *and* keep you with me. And look what happened to you. I ain't about to make the same mistake twice, Nas. You and Butta are all there is for me. A nigga like me ain't got no forgiveness coming to him. Ain't nothing after this life—I done did too much shit. I have to make the most of where I am right now, which means never letting you go again. I ain't never gon have you feeling like you don't belong. You hear me?"

"Vino," Nasima whispered, reaching up to touch his walnut face. She stroked the hard line of his jaw, ran her thumb over his full bottom lip, fingered the strong ridge of his cheekbone as she looked into his eyes. "I'm here, baby. You're not going to lose me again. I know I belong with you, and it has nothing to do with a damn bathroom. I know what I went through was hard, but you're letting it weigh on your heart like it was your fault when it wasn't. Trevino, we can't change what happened. But the happier you make me, the more I'm letting the past go. Please let it go too."

Vino swooped down, kissing her, stealing her breath and ravaging her mouth. Nasima kissed him back, took his worry, and gave her love in return. When he lifted his head, she was panting, and he stared at her, unsmiling. But he wasn't frowning.

"I love you," he whispered. He reached for Bashir's hand, brought them all in together. "Both of you."

"We know, Trev. But you can't control everything, and you're gonna make yourself sick trying. We need you the same way you need us. You gotta stop trying to take on every problem. The point of us being a unit is we learn how to solve things together," Bashir said.

Nasima nodded. She could feel Vino's every emotion, and her heart felt full.

"Okay," Trevino conceded with a nod. "So, what are we gonna do about the bathroom?"

"Nothing," Nasima laughed, twisting out of his arms, "because it's not a big deal. When I want to be with my boys, I will. And when I want to shower without somebody trying to make me come, I'll go next door."

She left the room, and her two men laughed as they followed.

Bashir

Bashir watched Nasima walk ahead of him, thanking God for ass and thighs and his gorgeous fat mama. Her jeans were plastered to her like a second skin, and her top showed a bit of belly and some of her back as she moved. She was a goddess in her pink sweater and dark wash jeans, and his hands itched with the need to touch her.

He held her coat as the three of them walked into his boxing gym, a part of him nervous about what she'd think. He'd upgraded quite a bit from the old days, and he wanted Nas to be impressed. The rubber flooring was yellow and black square tiles placed in a checkerboard pattern, and the bottom of the ring was draped in gray to match the walls. The ropes of the ring were yellow while the poles were black. Everything was top of the line and kept in great condition by his two managers.

"Oh, wow. Bash, it's beautiful." She turned to him, her face alight with wonder. He grinned as his heart went back to its normal pace. She liked it. All was right with the world. He took her hand.

"Let me show you everything, Lil Baby," he said, suddenly excited. Trev laughed softly behind him, amused at how eager he was. Bashir had been just as eager with him. They'd christened every inch of this place before it reopened, and Trevino let him know he thought it was a masterpiece as they made love over and over. He walked Nasima further inside and stopped. Trevino took the coats from him so both hands were free.

"This is our main area," he said, gesturing to the open room full of men, women, and teenagers training. "We have our main ring in the center, and beyond it, our heavy bags. Some are hanging, some are freestanding. Speed bag area is beyond it, and then the bathrooms. The two offices off to this right side are for Linc and Bunky—they run the day-to-day for me. In the next room, we have two smaller rings, some punching bag towers, which are basically an immobile sparring partner, and two enclosed areas—the weight room and the relaxation room."

"Relaxation room?" Nasima turned to him, curious.

"Yeah, babe. You gotta understand, when a lot of these people come in here, their worlds are out of control. They're looking for a way to focus the pain and work out the anger. Boxing helps, but after so much adrenaline, they need a way to come down. The relaxation space has yoga mats, candles and music for meditation, a couple of those electric massage chairs, and even an area for naps. I want everyone to be calm when they leave here. We train them to concentrate and express themselves, not to fight in the street."

"I love the way you sound when you talk about this," Nasima said, smiling hard. "I can tell you're so committed, and I love your joy in helping people process their emotions. You're so strong, Bash."

"I'm strong partly because of all the time I spent here." He smiled back, looking around with satisfaction. "That's why I needed to pay it forward."

"I'm so proud of you," she continued, leaning in close and rubbing his arm. "This is amazing. Plus, I love seeing so many young people here. This was a safe haven for kids when we were growing up, and I can tell it still is."

"I'm so happy you like it," Bashir said, feeling giddy. His heart was full to bursting as he looked into Nasima's eyes. Seeing her know more of him and hearing her say she was proud moved something in him. His fingers tingled, his dick woke up, and his mouth was dry. He needed her in his arms.

He wanted to hold her forever and make sure she never stopped looking at him the way she was now.

Bashir released his breath. Only Trev ever made him feel this way. Was he in love with Nasima already? The air was charged around them, but as he filled his lungs, he knew he'd never felt so restored, so full of life. And she was the reason. Nasima was lifting him, freshening his perspective, fortifying him. Bashir pulled her to his chest, leaned down, and kissed her gently.

"Don't you start nothing in here," she warned playfully, stepping away from him with a laugh. Bashir laughed too, and the two of them headed to find Trevino.

Trev was in the next room, speaking softly to a man Bashir recognized as Easy, one of King's lieutenants. He and three others were Trev's direct reports and kept the operation secure so he didn't have to work every day. Back when Nasima was around and the operation was first coming together, Trev did all the wet work, all the defense planning, and all enforcement logistics. Romelo simply didn't trust anyone else. But things had changed. King had a strong core of men who were loyal not only to him, but to Trevino also, which left Trev to handle the heavy-duty work. Easy nodded his head, smirking. Bashir knew Trev was giving him instructions.

"Oh good, there y'all are. Lil Baby, come here. Bet you don't remember—"

"Elliott? Is that you?" Nasima said, running into Easy's arms. Her hug nearly knocked him over, but he recovered, holding her tightly and laughing.

"Girl, you out here throwing my government around. They call me Easy now. How you been, Nas?" Easy said.

Nasima laughed with him, reaching up to touch his face. "I'm much better since I'm back with my Vino. I missed you. I'm glad you're okay. How is everything with you?"

"I'm cool, boo. Nothing major going on. Making money and making sure Truck and King get where they need to go."

"Always the watcher. It's what you're best at. You've been the eyes since we were kids," Nasima observed. Easy grinned, his chest puffing up at her compliment. He held her hand, falling under her spell, and Bashir found himself feeling something he'd never thought he'd feel with Nas: jealousy.

"We grew up together, Butta. Fix your face," Trevino whispered, coming up next to him, and Bashir checked himself, fixing his face and releasing the urge to get his woman's hand out of Easy's...by force if necessary. He looked away, and Trevino bit his lip to keep from laughing.

"Come by the house one Sunday, Nas. MomMom would love to see you," Easy said, referring to the grandmother who'd raised him. "You can even bring these two. Trev still gets on her nerves, but she loves Bash."

Nasima laughed and turned to look at them, happiness in her whiskey eyes.

"Okay. Maybe in a couple of weeks," she agreed. Easy hugged her again, excited. He took his leave after, stopping to verify a couple of things with Trev before leaving the gym. Trevino sighed, reached in his pocket for his second cell phone, and turned it on.

Bashir went still. He knew what the second phone meant: Trev was working later, probably all night. It was his first time having all-night work since Nasima had been with them, and Bashir could feel the angst coming off him because he was worried how she'd take it.

"Let's look around some more, then we can get something to eat," he said, and Nasima grabbed both their hands, eager for the rest of the tour. After another half-hour, Bashir grabbed their coats from the office and checked in with Linc and Bunky. Then the three of them got into his Range Rover and headed to a restaurant.

Trevino

There was no easy way to tell Lil Baby he had to work tonight. His boys had sniffed out a rat or two, and King needed to know what they knew and who they'd told. Easy, ever the observer, got the drop on the two niggas picking up dry cleaning, of all things. They were tied up at the warehouse waiting for him. They'd keep until tonight, but not longer. Which meant he had four hours to tell Nasima he was working and deal with the fallout.

Back in the day, his night work came between them more than anything else. Her worry over his safety and her guilt over her worry triggering his and fucking with his concentration was juxtaposed against his guilt over her worry and his worry over her being alone crying about him. At least tonight, she wouldn't be alone. Trevino thanked God for Butta, his rock, who he knew loved Nasima too. Butta would take care of her...if she stayed. Thoughts of the alternative raced through Trevino's mind, fucked up his appetite. What if being this up close and personal with his work was too much for Nasima, triggered her somehow? What if it made her want to leave?

"Vino, whatever has you so upset, please tell me. I can feel it all over me," Nasima finally said, putting her fork down. Bashir looked between them, silent but curious. Trevino sighed. Sometimes he forgot how connected they were.

"I have work tonight...all night," he said. Nasima looked at him, fear coming into her eyes. Trevino pushed his plate away. He hated that look.

"You haven't been working all night before this. Why tonight? Why during our special time—"

"I've been moving things around as best I can. I wanted to have more time to ease you into this. But I don't, Lil Baby, and I'm sorry. I can't procrastinate anymore. King needs me to do what I do, so I'm going," he explained.

Romelo had questioned whether he was shirking his responsibilities for a reason. When Trevino explained the reason was Nasima, he was more understanding but still firm. They couldn't sit on these niggas indefinitely, and they needed information to protect themselves—and counterattack if necessary. Truck Davis was on the clock.

"Can I call you, or text you?" Nasima asked, her bottom lip quivering. If she cried, Trevino was done. He shook his head.

"For your protection, we're no-contact—nothing's changed. I'm going to give you Romelo's housekeeper's number, which is what Butta has. If something happens the two of you can't handle alone, call her. She can get a message to me," he explained. Nasima closed her eyes and shook her head.

"I know I should be used to this. I should—"

"Nas, you don't have to be used to anything. Look at how long we were apart. I'm not expecting you to fit right back into this aspect of my life, especially since you had trouble with it before too. Feel however you want to feel. You want to be angry with me? That's okay too, baby. The only thing I need is for you to stay. Don't leave. I can't bear it if you...you can shut yourself up in the room and not speak to me, walk around with an attitude, tell me I can't touch you, whatever you need. But you can't leave."

"Vino, I don't want my fear to be a distraction. You need focus, and I—"

"You're not a distraction, Lil Baby."

"I am if you're more worried about me crying as you walk out the door than you are about getting the work done!" she said.

"Then you won't cry." Bashir stepped in, his eyes a little tortured as he stared at the two of them arguing. "I'm here with you now, Nas. We'll have a night to ourselves; we'll do whatever you want. I'll remind you Trev is the best there is, and he's undefeated. We'll sleep in each other's arms, and when we wake up, he'll be home."

"You shouldn't have to baby me—"

"Why shouldn't I? This is all a part of us becoming a unit. It's part of me wanting to be your man too. The only reason you cried alone back then was because Trev didn't trust anyone with you but himself. But I'm here now," Bashir said.

"And I trust Butta with my life, and yours," Trevino said, reaching across the table for Nasima's hands. She held them out willingly, her fingers gripping him so tightly. "Hold onto him. Let him hold onto you. And I'll be home to make you breakfast, Lil Baby. I promise."

He looked into Nasima's whiskey eyes and fell even deeper in love, though he didn't know how it was possible. She was his heart in human form, the reason he opened his life up to find Bashir in the first place. He refused to lose her. Hopefully, Bashir's devotion to her and their new dynamic would be enough to convince her to stay, ease into this new normal with them, and sleep peacefully until he came home. Nasima let go of one of his hands to hold Bashir's.

"I want French toast," she said quietly, and Trevino and Butta laughed. The tension was broken, and his appetite was back. Now, to spend some quality time with his loves before Truck Davis had to clock in.

"Lil Baby, come here for a second," Trevino called to Nasima from the walk-in closet in their bedroom. Nasima walked in and out again, confused.

"Vino? I thought you were in here."

"I am, baby. Come back further. Walk past the hoodies and turn," he directed her.

When she found him, she gasped. The closet had a hidden door; it pushed back into a mini armory for Trevino. He had most of his weapons stockpiled at the apartment, but there were some here too because he refused to be vulnerable. Nasima walked into the little room, staring at the guns mounted on the wall and the containers of bullets beneath them, cases of assorted knives and tasers, and even clubs and bats hanging up. He knew it was overwhelming for her, but he needed to let her know there was protection here.

"Vino, this is...wow," she said, still wide-eyed. Trevino smiled and took her hand.

"Put your thumb here," he instructed, pulling out the hidden keypad on the door and pressing her thumb into it. When the print was scanned, Trevino entered a code, and the print was saved.

"What did you just do?"

"Made sure you could get in here if you needed to. Now, don't be upset. I'm not trying to scare you. But I do have to prepare you, Nas. I survive because I anticipate—you know who I am. If you're ever in trouble, you come past the hoodies and pull this empty hook. The entry pad will pop out, and when you scan your thumb, the door will open. I'm not asking you to use anything in here. If you need it to hide, then hide. But I need you to know you can get in here, okay?" Trevino said.

Nasima nodded, swallowing nervously. "Okay, Vino," she whispered. He pulled her close and kissed her hair. She was probably remembering their safety protocols from when they were young. Nasima didn't live with him back then, but she was with him so much she might as well have. They had a system then too. It was much cruder; he wasn't working with as much money back then. But he would have done anything to keep Nas safe, and he would now.

The two of them went back into the bedroom and snuggled into bed with Bashir, sharing dessert and watching TV. Soon, Trevino got up and changed. It was time. Nasima wrapped herself around his waist, her softness centering him. He squeezed her tight, kissed her hard.

"French toast in the morning, okay?" he whispered to her. Nasima nodded.

"You're my heart walking around, Vino. You come home in one piece; don't break my heart," she said back. He nodded. She got back into bed, and he grabbed Bashir's hand and left the room. They went downstairs and to the door. Trevino pulled his man close and kissed him passionately, their tongues and lips intense. When he pulled back, Butta looked at him with wonder and lust in his eyes.

"I love you," Trevino said.

"I love you too. I'll give you a few minutes with Nas first in the morning, okay?" Butta said.

Trevino nodded. "Good. Don't forget to take something for your headache, and don't sleep with the TV on."

"Okay, babe," Butta said, laughing. "You need anything else from me before you go to work?"

Trevino reached down, grabbed Butta's dick, and started rubbing it into hardness. "I need you to go upstairs and work too, you hear me?" he said, moving his hand up and down faster. Bashir moaned and closed his eyes. "You hear me, Butta? I don't want her up all night worrying. Take my dick up there and do work. Put her ass to sleep."

"Okay, baby, I got you," Bashir agreed, thrusting his hips forward, eager for more touches. Trevino rubbed him once more, kissed him again, and was out the door. He got into his car, pulled out his phone. King was ready.

Trevino nodded. Truck was ready too.

Bashir

Bashir waited until the door shut behind Trevino before heading back upstairs. When he got to the bedroom, Nasima was in bed, curled into a ball, staring at the TV. He got into bed with her and pulled her closer, turning her to face him.

"You good?" he asked. Nasima nodded, but her eyes were scared, and her mouth was pouting. Bashir kissed her, pressing his lips against hers, making her relax against him. Her arms went around his neck, and she kissed him back, moaning softly. His hands went under her shirt and grabbed her soft belly. Nasima pulled back, staring at him.

"What do you normally do after he leaves?" she asked him. Bashir smirked.

"I eat without sharing with his greedy ass, and I go to sleep." After he answered, Nasima giggled in surprise. Bashir knew she wasn't expecting his response.

"Were you always this calm about what he does? Didn't it ever bother you?" she asked next.

"It bothers me now, Nas," he said, "I'm not completely unaffected. But I shift the way I think about it so I can rest, and so he can work. I tell myself Trev is the best, he has backup, and he wants to come home in one piece as much as I want him to. I remind myself he's thought of every possible outcome, run every scenario through his head. And I know he has because, again, he's the best."

"He survives because he anticipates." Nasima repeated Trevino's words to her. Bashir nodded.

"It helps me put it in perspective. It'll help you too, babe. It's your first time doing this in years. You'll be fine, and I'm not going anywhere," Bashir said. Nasima smiled, and he felt her body relax against him.

"Can we get a snack?" she asked. Bashir nodded, laughing. Ten minutes later, they were down in the kitchen, listening to oldies and pulling things out of the fridge. They snacked on leftover tuna salad with crackers, baby carrots with hummus, and chocolate cookies. After the food, they danced to The Temptations while reminiscing about the movie. Bashir loved seeing the light come back into Nasima's eyes, loved how she was leaning into him. He could tell she was still worried, but a short reprieve was better than none.

An hour later, the two of them were back upstairs. Bashir kissed Nasima's mouth, rubbed her softness, tried to get her body to fully ease, but her mind was mired in worry, and it was no use. Trev's gonna be annoyed, he thought, but there was no help for it. Bashir wouldn't try to force her to be into it.

"How did you meet Vino?" she asked, snuggling into his arms. They were sitting up in bed now, and she was reading a book while he watched TV. Bashir smiled.

"I didn't meet Trev, he met me," he said. Nasima laughed and looked up at him. "I knew who he was, of course. And I was crushing on him hard. But I wasn't gonna do anything about it. He heard about all the fights I was getting into—coming out made a lot of niggas think they could talk to me any kind of way, and I wasn't having it—and one day, he pulled up when I was breaking this nigga's jaw. He put a gun to his head, told him and everyone watching I was off-limits, for good. I was mad as hell."

"Why? Wait, I know—you wanted to fight your own battles," Nasima said. Bashir nodded.

"Yeah, Lil Baby. Having Truck on your side is a big deal, but I didn't want him thinking I needed to be saved. Turns out, it was his way of flirting with me."

"Sounds like Vino," Nasima said, and the two of them laughed.

"And what about you? He's had you since diapers, right?"

"Yup. Our moms were best friends at one point. They fell off, but we never did. And eventually my parents were too busy getting high to even remember they had a daughter, so Vino protected me. After high school, I went to community college, majored in Business and Accounting. Vino paid for it. Then he started saying I should start a new life somewhere else, get away from the legacy of this place. I didn't want to leave him, but I knew he was right. I tried to get him to come with me, but—"

"He was already too deep in the streets to walk away," Bashir finished for her. Nasima nodded.

"He wasn't going to leave Romelo; it was too late. I left my best friend, my only love, and I missed him so much."

"But you know he was right, don't you, Nas? No matter how it turned out, you needed the chance to have a life. Leaving was the right thing to do."

"I know it was," she whispered, "and he found you. He found something real, which was all I wanted for him."

"And now we've found each other," Bashir said softly, leaning down to kiss her again. "You have something real again too. Trev is here, and so am I. You can let your guard down and be happy, baby. I promise you it's real."

"How is this happening so fast, Bash? How do I feel so much with you, so soon?"

"Because it's meant to be, Lil Baby. And I feel it too," he promised her, holding her tightly until they both drifted off to sleep.

Chapter 5

Trevino

Trevino entered the code on the keypad at his front door and walked inside. He dropped his bag on the bench in the entryway and sighed deeply. It was a typical night, but Nasima's worry made it feel heavier.

He tried to shake it off, push it down. He did what he had to do. Trevino knew he was a grimy nigga who relished the dirt on his hands, who didn't feel the blood on his soul. He didn't question his work and he didn't apologize. Butta was used to it, used to him, and his lover didn't judge. But maybe Nasima would. The look in those brown eyes when he walked out of the room stuck with him all night. She was afraid for him, fearful of his demise. And for the first time in a long time, it was getting to him.

"Good morning, Vino."

Her soft voice pierced the silence. The darkness outside was making way for light, the sky moving from black into a dirty gray, the sun waiting for its sign to peek through. Trevino looked up. The open floor plan of their home allowed him to see straight into the kitchen, where Nasima was sitting on the island, feet swinging, big thighs open. Her hands were flat on the island, like she was bracing herself, and her breath came in short bursts, making her big titties heave and her fat belly jiggle under the shirt she was wearing.

He smiled and took off his jacket and t-shirt. His boots went next, and he went to her, closing the distance between her body and his hands as fast as he could. Butta was going to kill him for leaving all his shit on the floor, but he couldn't take one more second of their separation. He had to get to Nasima. Trevino grabbed her thighs, pulled her forward, folded her into his body. Nasima sighed, her relief so palpable he felt it in his own bones. She buried her face in his chest, sniffing him, her body starting to quiver.

"I'm home, Lil Baby. Vino's home," he soothed her, whispering in her ear. Nasima kissed his chest and dug her fingers into his sides. He relished her touch, fell into her love. She was still settling into their new love, but he knew it was real. Nas was theirs—his and Butta's—and if the previous week hadn't proved it, this welcome home certainly did. Another person would have left them, taken their fear under their arm like a playground ball and gone home. Another person wouldn't have tried to handle it. The two others who'd shared their home were kept in the dark as much as possible for fear they *couldn't* handle it. Trevino thanked the universe for Nas—and for Butta, who he knew left Nasima here to welcome him home alone. He knew she needed a moment with him to herself.

Nasima pulled back, tilting her head to look into his eyes.

"H-how was work?" she whispered. Trevino chuckled, the sound muffled against her forehead as he kissed her there. She smelled like baby powder and roses with traces of weed and Butta's body wash, and he knew she'd spent the night in Bashir's arms. As a man who did his work under the cover of night, he was glad neither of them ever had to sleep alone again.

"You don't have to ask about it, Lil Baby," he assured her. "I don't tell Butta, and I won't tell you. You don't need to know what happened; you just need to know I'm home."

"I'm glad you're home," Nasima said, leaning into his chest again. "You want some breakfast?"

"I want some pussy," he replied bluntly, "and I want to hold onto you. I know you need me too." Trevino backed up and helped her down from the island, letting her go in front of him so he could watch her ass sway as they went upstairs.

"You don't want to speak to Bashir?" Nasima asked, turning back to him. He slapped her behind—hard.

"You worry about where you supposed to be. Butta knows we need a minute to ourselves. It's why he left you there to meet me. Now get your ass upstairs."

She obeyed without further questions, and soon, they were in the bedroom, lips and tongues meeting with passion. Trevino licked her mouth, tasted her thoroughly, gripped her soft body in his hands. He pushed Nasima back onto the bed, watching as she squirmed under his gaze.

"I'm gonna shower real quick, Lil Baby," he said, winking at her. He went into the en suite, ridding himself of the rest of his clothing quickly and hopping into the shower. A quick but rigorous wash and he was out again, pulling a new towel from the shelf and drying himself. When he reentered the bedroom, Nasima was lying on her side, clenching her thighs together, her elbow up, her face leaning into her palm. She licked her lips as she stared at him, those whiskey eyes filling with desire for him—and happiness.

"How was your shower?" she asked him. Trevino smirked and got down next to her on the bed, pushing her onto her back and moving between her thighs.

"Next time, bring your ass in there with me and stop acting like you need my permission to be where I am. We not beefing; you don't need to be nervous. You were upset about me going to work, but now I'm home. We're us. What I tell you about that, Nas?"

"I...you can take your shower in peace, Vino. You're home now, like you said; I don't mind waiting for you," Nasima tried to reason. He leaned down and nipped her chin, sinking his teeth into her neck. Her sharp exhalation was his permission; he sucked her flesh into his mouth, not caring to be soft, the harshness of his kisses a lesson she needed to learn.

"You and Butta *are* my peace. When I walk in this door, you can cling to me as tightly as you want," he said, his voice a mumble as he continued to bite her neck. Nasima moaned, arching her body into him, her eyes shutting. Trevino leaned up and pulled his shirt over her head, smiling inside at her need to be close to him in any way she could. He pulled up to his knees and tugged her lounging shorts off, making a note to throw them away later. He didn't need barriers between her body and theirs anymore; Nasima could walk around naked for all he cared. This was her home, their sanctuary. Nothing was more important than her comfort—hers and Butta's. He was the provider, and he took it seriously.

Trevino groaned when he realized she remembered his edict and wasn't wearing panties. He saw her fat pussy, hairs glistening with her arousal, lips plump and perfect.

Spreading her wide, he sank inside with no preliminaries. There was no place like home.

Nasima whimpered, accepted him, her eyes opening to slits as she stared up at him. She bit her lower lip and he thrust hard, his desire for her spilling over. Trevino leaned down again, caught a nipple between his teeth, and tugged. Nasima cried out, the pain sharp, the pleasure sharper. He licked her to soothe the sting, suckled her properly, and she dug her nails into his shoulders.

"You miss me, Nas?" he asked in a gruff whisper around a mouthful of breast. She nodded, taking his dick like a champ, her wetness creating a rhythmic, juicy, smacking sound as he fucked her.

"Yes, baby. I missed you—so much. All night—Vino!"

"I'm right here, Lil Baby," he said, releasing her breast and kissing her mouth, "and now I gotta cuss Butta's ass out."

"Wha-what? Why?" Nasima asked, her pussy running over as he filled it again and again. Trevino moved his hips, thrusting hard, bottoming out in her wet paradise. He almost couldn't think, she was so sexy. Her scent wafted up around them; her cries filled the silence of the room. He continued fucking her, his balls tightening with the need to come.

"Because," he said, moving in and out, "if you missed me all night, then that nigga wasn't on his job. I told him to put you to sleep."

"It-it wasn't him, baby. I-I was too worried. Ooooh shit, Vino!" Nasima defended Bashir and then came, her pussy clenching him and wetting them both. Trevino cursed under his breath and moaned into her neck, hoping he could keep from coming too. He needed to wear her ass out.

"She was too in her head, Trev. Worrying over you. I ended up holding her and talking to her," Bashir said, entering the room. They both looked over at him, his light brown skin still dotted with water from his shower in the downstairs bathroom. Trevino smiled at his man, licked his lips.

"Then come drop some dick in her mouth so she can make it up to you," he directed. Bashir got on the bed, coming up next to Nasima's head and getting on his knees. He stared at her affectionately.

"Told you he was coming home," he said. Nasima nodded, still coming down from her orgasm, a new fire in her eyes.

"I'm sorry I doubted you, Bash," she said, her tongue darting out to wet her lower lip. Bashir took his heavy dick in his hands and swiped the tip over her lips.

"Show me," he ordered, and Nasima opened her mouth fully, taking his head and sucking. Bashir sighed, sliding more of himself into her throat. He fucked her mouth gently and Trevino pressed his hands into Nasima's thighs, fucking her pussy hard. She whimpered as they both filled her, her titties bouncing, saliva leaking from the corners of her mouth.

"I don't know what's sexier," Trevino said, "watching them jaws work or watching these big, pretty ass titties bouncing." Nasima moaned in response, lapping at the underside of Bashir's dick with her tongue, her pussy leaking onto the bed. Trevino sped up his thrusts, his head spinning as he drowned in her ocean. Nasima's pussy was top-tier and watching her give head was taking him there even faster.

Bashir was groaning, his head thrown back, his spine rigid. Nasima added her hands, massaging and squeezing his balls as she sucked him. The sight of her, two holes filled, running wetter than a rainstorm had Trevino moaning. Then he glanced at his Butta, his other lover, on the verge of nutting right into her throat, and couldn't help it anymore. With a growl, Trevino let loose, his nut shooting into Nasima's pussy. His release triggered hers, and she squirted, moaning around a mouthful of dick as she came for the third time.

Bashir grabbed her titty, tugged her nipple, and cried out as he shot his seed into her throat. Nasima swallowed him, drank him greedily, the leftovers running down the sides of her mouth. Bashir pulled away and fell onto the bed, his breathing ragged. Trevino pulled out, going to the other side so Nasima was sandwiched between them. He used the shirt she was wearing to wipe her mouth and kissed her, tasting her and Butta, feeling like he was home.

"I'm not sleeping in this wet spot," she pouted when he released her mouth.

Trevino laughed. He leaned over and kissed Bashir as well, sucking on his bottom lip and making him moan a little. He lay back down, pulling them both against him.

"Your ass the one who made it. Why wouldn't you have to sleep there?"

"Ain't no sleep yet, anyway. I fully intend to fuck both of you again, and then we'll need a shower. New sheets can come after," Bashir said. Trevino shrugged. Fine by him.

"By then, we'll want to nap, and I'll make us food when we wake up," Nasima said.

The two men looked at her, surprised. It was the first time they heard Nas speak like she was a part of their household and not a guest. They both moved in, squeezing her tightly. Trevino kissed her hair, Bashir her forehead. Trevino guessed surviving a night of him going to work was making her feel like she did belong. Her need to express her fear and stay to reconnect with them instead of simply leaving convinced her there was something more there than what she'd thought. Nasima drifted off first, and he took a moment to check in with his other love.

"I'm happy to see you, Butta. Good morning, love," Trevino whispered.

"Good morning to you, babe. Glad you're home," Bashir whispered back, smiling.

"How was she?" Trevino asked, gesturing to their pretty fat mama asleep between them. Bashir shrugged.

"She handled it much better than she'll give herself credit for. And we got to talk a lot, which we both loved."

"Good. Thank you, Butta. Thank you for holding down our home."

"It's my pleasure, babe. We're complete, and so is our home. I love holding you down," Bashir said.

Trevino looked into his lover's big, brown eyes and gave thanks for so much patience and understanding. He was a hard man who often questioned whether he deserved so much softness and love, whether he would even know how to treat it, cultivate it. Bashir made him run into it eagerly and try. After he lost Nasima, he didn't think anyone would. And now he had them both. But a man like Butta was rare, and Trevino didn't take it for granted.

He leaned up to kiss him again. Bashir met his lips, and they both sighed with pleasure before settling down again. Trevino took a deep breath, content. The air expanded his lungs, reminding him he was alive. He snuggled closer, knowing the ease was him starting to feel whole. It was Bashir and Nasima, making them whole.

Bashir

Bashir never thought of himself as someone who craved pussy. Sure, he liked it, had even loved it at times. And he could wear it out when he got ready; his stroke game was damn good. But he'd never thought of himself as someone who craved it, thirsted for it, was hell bent on having it.

And then he met Nasima Jones. He caught her scent and was immediately addicted. He'd damn near die for the taste of her, and she acted like she didn't even know it. Walking around their home hesitant, afraid to speak her wants, afraid to demand her pleasure. The smell of her could turn both him and Trev into full-blown sex slaves, and Bashir found himself needing to make Nasima aware of her power. His tongue did a full lap from her asshole to her clit, catching the wetness of her desire and swirling around her swollen nub before sucking it into his mouth. Nasima's loud moans filled the room, her lower body squirming as she tried to get away from the onslaught of his lips and tongue.

Bashir laughed. Her ass wasn't going anywhere. She was lying against Trevino's chest, her arms held down by his bigger ones as he played with her nipples. The double stimulation had Nasima's eyes rolling back in her head, the pleasure almost too much.

"Bash—baby, please! I—"

"Hold still and let me eat, Nas." Bashir ignored her and went back to his licking, holding her thighs in place and tasting her pussy slowly. He kissed her lips, pushed his tongue between, slurped her juices, and sucked on her clit until tears were running down her cheeks.

"Bash, I can't take it. I can't—"

"Come one more time for me, Lil Baby," Bashir insisted and swirled his tongue between her slick folds. He was focused, obsessed, consumed with the need to please her...and let her know how much pleasing her pleased him. He moaned, his tongue lethal, trying to catch every drop of her cream. Nasima sobbed, her body jerked, and she squirted into his mouth. He swallowed every drop as her breath caught, and she was suspended between rapture and incoherence. Her eyes shut and her body went still.

"Breathe, mama," Trev said, kissing her cheeks and nose, "we're not gonna let you go. Me and Butta are right here. Breathe with us."

Nasima gasped, opening her eyes again, freeing her arms and pushing Bashir's head away.

"No more, baby," she pushed out on a whimper, "please, no more."

Bashir sat up, licking the last of her from his mouth. He moved beside Trevino, pulling Nasima onto his lap.

"You did so good, Nas," he praised her, kissing her chubby cheeks and rubbing her body. There was so much of her to hold onto, and he loved it all. Nasima snuggled closer, still slightly shaking. Trevino got up and went to the other side of the room, coming back with cold water and a small bowl of strawberries. Bashir took the water and tilted the bottle to her mouth, making sure she was taking healthy sips.

When her breathing was back to normal, she took the bowl of strawberries, feeding them each one before eating two herself. The three of them relaxed for a moment, then Nasima moved, getting off the bed and heading into the bathroom. Bashir sighed, a smile on his face. Trevino leaned over and took his mouth, his kiss urgent and hard. Bashir kissed him back, their tongues thrashing against each other. Kissing Trevino Davis never got old. It was still the same fire, the same perfect, passionate moment—the same love.

Bashir moved closer, moaned low in his throat. He wanted his man to fill him up.

"Fuck me, Trev," he whispered. Trevino growled, his hands reaching.

"You ain't gotta ask me, Butta; I was gon do that anyway," he whispered back. The two continued kissing as Trevino reached back and fumbled with the nightstand drawer, grabbing a bottle of lube. Bashir finally pulled his mouth away, looking up at Nasima. She was staring at them, her gaze tired but still hungry, as if he hadn't nearly made her pass out shortly before.

"Come lay underneath me, Lil Baby, so I can kiss you," Bashir said. Nasima climbed into bed, lying on her back, and spread her thighs. Bashir got between them, kissing her stomach and going into his arch. He felt the cool slickness of the lube over his asshole and then two of Trevino's thick fingers inside of him.

"Oooh shit. Yes, Trev," he said, staring into Nasima's eyes as he spoke. He needed her to see how important she was to their connection. He needed to breathe. And he could only do it when he was looking into her whiskey eyes.

Trevino used his fingers to stretch Bashir's anus, getting him ready. Then, the fingers were gone, and Trev's thick dick pushed inside, inch by inch. Bashir took deep breaths, kissing Nasima on her breasts and stomach as he stared into her eyes. When Trevino was in fully, they both moaned.

"Fuck, Butta. This ass is so tight and perfect," he said, holding still so they could both get their bearings. Nasima held Bashir's face in her hands and smiled.

"You look so beautiful like this," she whispered, "both of you so powerful, so vulnerable. I love looking at you."

Her words made them both smile, and Trevino started to move, pulling out slightly and sliding in again. Soon, they were fucking faster, their rhythm perfect after five years. Bashir used one hand to jerk his hard dick and muffled some of his moans with mouthfuls of Nasima's nipples. She watched them, fascinated with their connection, took his kisses, and sucked on his tongue.

"Trev, shit. Oh fuck, yes." Bashir praised his lover as only he could, feeling his thick dick touch places no one else had ever gone. Trevino was never rough (unless you asked him to be) but he was always determined, always ready to give you whatever you needed. Bashir never had a lover be so dominant while also being so ridiculously generous, and there was no doubt it was love. Trevino thrust in and out, threw his head back, slapped Bashir's ass as he got further into his rhythm. Bashir gripped his dick, felt his nut rising, licked at Nasima's nipples again. She whimpered and her thighs clenched, and he knew she came again while watching them. Bashir moaned loud and came in his palm, his nut shooting out in spurts.

"Fuck!" Trevino shouted and shot his load into Bashir's ass, gripping him by the waist to steady himself. He pulled out, stumbling back, and fell to the side, spent. Bashir collapsed on top of Nasima, murmuring her name. She rubbed his head to calm him, kissing his sweaty forehead.

"I'm right here, baby," she whispered, "I'm right here."

The three of them slept in their sticky, sweaty mess and woke up ready for a shower. Their en suite was only really big enough for two, but they made it work and managed to curtail their sexual appetites for their actual ones. The bedroom refresh was fast because they worked together, and Bashir dropped their linens in the laundry before meeting

Trev and Nas in the kitchen. The men opted for boxers and nothing else and finally convinced Nasima to ease into her comfort and simply wear a t-shirt. She made them all a quick shrimp pasta dish with pesto, and they sat down to eat together, famished after rounds of lovemaking.

"This shit is good, Lil Baby. Where you learn to cook like this?" Bashir asked. Nasima giggled at the compliment.

"I used to take classes. Cooking is relaxing to me; it became a hobby of mine. I'm glad you like it."

"You be cooking for them niggas at Smoke house like this?" Trevino demanded, inhaling his food. Nasima shrugged.

"When I first got there, I only cooked for myself. But then they started noticing my food and asking for it. Smoke said since I was the best cook in the house, I should cook for everybody. I didn't want to, but I didn't really feel like I could say no, you know? It's his place, and he did me a favor, letting me stay there," she explained.

"So, they're taking advantage of you? Of your kindness?" Trevino said.

Nasima's eyes widened, and she reached for Trev, hoping to calm him down. "Vino, it's not like that. Don't be mad. I don't mind it now, I really don't. I haven't been able to take any classes in a while, so cooking for other people helps me decompress and keep my skills sharp."

Trevino's eyes narrowed, and Bashir shook his head slightly. This wasn't the time for Truck Davis to come out. Trev sighed and went back to his food. Bashir reached for Nasima's hand, squeezing it.

"You ain't gotta worry about it no more, Nas. You only gotta feed us if you *want* to. Find the classes and we'll take care of it, okay?" he told her.

Nasima shook her head like she couldn't believe it. "Oh no, y'all don't have to—"

"You ours, Lil Baby. You belong to me and Butta now. And we belong to you. Don't tell us we don't have to take care of you. We're men, and we're *your* men—yes, the fuck we do," Trevino said with finality.

Bashir smirked. When Trev wants something, you better give it to him, he thought. Even if it's your heart. Nasima sat there, speechless. Then she leaned over, pulling Trev's face from his bowl and kissing his lips soundly.

"I see Truck Davis in your eyes. Don't you hurt him over me," she told him, referring to her cousin. Trevino smirked.

"Ain't nothing you can do about what I'm a do to him, babe. You gotta let it be. I know you don't want to, but I need you to."

Nasima nodded in understanding and came over to Bashir, kissing his lips as well. Then they finished eating. After food, Nasima wanted to sprawl on the couch and watch TV, and they obliged her. Trevino's night of work finally caught up with him and he was asleep in minutes. Bashir snuggled between the two of them on the couch, holding each of them to his side, breathing deep.

Nasima

Nasima sat at the vanity in the guest bedroom, combing out her hair. It was past her shoulders now, but still thinner than she wanted due to genetics and stress. She'd started this great treatment with a stylist when she was in her old place...before she was forced back here by life and cheating ass niggas.

She took a deep breath and pushed the melancholy away. There was no point in it now. She learned a valuable lesson from Tone, one she would never forget or repeat. What happened, happened—and now she was in an entirely new situation; it was different from everything she'd ever known, but somehow felt righter than anything else she'd done. The pull of this neighborhood, these old, inhabited memories, would never be enough. And when Nasima came back here, she knew formulating a plan to leave again was her only move.

But now she was fully immersed and feeling happy. Nasima could admit it was Trevino. She'd known, deep down, since he came into her life when they were kids, that things would begin and end with him at her side, and he'd known it too. And now he'd given her a bonus—Bashir on the other side. Two men, at her feet, belonging to themselves, and to each other, and to her all at once. It was heady and scary, and Nasima couldn't believe she was free falling like this. But once again, it was Trevino, and everything with her and Vino felt like the inevitable. The last week had been a soft, warm, erotic dream. She'd been filled with food, with dick, with care and cum, and no one had ever anticipated her needs so well or worked so hard to fulfill them. But could she make a life? A love?

Nasima wasn't sure. As much as Vino and Bash told her she fit perfectly, and as much as having this dynamic was a part of her secret dream, Nasima couldn't help but wonder if it would all fall apart before she got to enjoy it, like everything else in her life.

"You can drop as many bags as you want at the mall tomorrow if you tell me what you're so worried about," Bashir said, entering the room.

Nasima turned to face him, still a little overwhelmed by how fine he was. His light skin glistened as he stood in the doorway, his face clear and smooth, his beard full but neatly trimmed. His low-cut fade and hairline were perfect —Trevino would never allow it to be any other way—and his smile was contagious. Although his height matched Vino's, his body was thicker, spongier, and she wanted to cuddle every time she looked at his bare chest. Bashir was a man you noticed, and with his gentle demeanor and calming ways, he made everything smoother, silkier, shinier. It was no wonder Vino called him Butta.

"You don't need to bribe me, Bash. I'll talk to you."

"And we were going to the mall even if you didn't tell me anything, so we're good. But enough of that—what's going on, Lil Baby?"

"I'm worried, Bashir. Things in my life have an annoying habit of falling apart as soon as I start getting used to them. I don't want that to happen with us."

"You don't need to worry, Nas. Those things fell apart because they weren't me and Trev, babe. With you, we're complete, and we'll do whatever we have to do to keep you with us. Those things fell apart because you didn't have someone else helping you fight for them. But you got us now," Bashir said, coming to stand behind her. His hands went to her shoulders, rubbing and pressing. Nasima moaned softly, relaxing into his hands.

"You make me feel so good," she whispered. Bashir kept up his massage, leaning down to kiss the top of her head.

"I know I don't have magic powers and I can't make all the fear go away," he whispered back, "but I'm going to ask you to do your best to trust me, Nas. Trust us. Don't let the fear take you over. Lay it on us, let us help you with it. When you need to be reassured, tell us. Don't sit here and let the doubt fester."

"I'm afraid you'll resent me for staying, for wanting to stay," Nasima blurted out, raising her eyes to his in the mirror. She hadn't meant to say her thoughts aloud, but with a man like Bash, it was almost impossible not to.

"I need more than that, Lil Baby," he said. "Explain yourself."

"I'm scared you'll eventually be upset at him sharing his heart with me. I'm scared you'll hate me because you're not the only person he loves anymore," she said, taking a deep breath after.

Bashir laughed softly, then he smiled so big she was dazed for a second. He spun her to face him, squatting down so they were eye level.

"Nasima," he started, moving her hair behind her ear and running a thumb across her lips, "you're a part of us now. There's enough love for everybody, and I am so sorry that useless nigga handled you wrong and made you feel like love wasn't infinite, like you would ever have to choose. Every piece Trev gives to you, I get back...from you. You're mine too, baby."

"Oh, Bash," Nasima whispered and threw her arms around his neck. He kissed her, running his hands over her body. She moaned into his mouth, feeling more of her reservations scatter like the wind blew over them. Bashir pulled away, kissing her nose and forehead.

"You really do share a heart with him," he said, chuckling again.

Nasima stared at him, her brows wrinkled in confusion. "What do you mean?"

"Me and Trev had a similar version of the same conversation. He needed a little reassurance, and so did I. But he was mostly worried about me, like you are. Y'all really in love with a nigga, huh?"

"I think I might be," Nasima whispered, kissing him again. The two were still lip-locked when Trevino walked in, chewing loudly, a blunt in one hand and a bowl full of fruit in the other.

"Y'all wanna smoke?" he said, not caring about his interruption.

Bashir stood up straight and grabbed Nasima's hand, pulling her from the chair. Nasima walked up to Trevino, smiling sweetly. Trevino grinned back, leaning down to nuzzle her neck.

"I don't want to smoke," she said, reaching back for Bashir's hand. He grabbed it, and she felt settled. Anchored. "You boys have fun, and I'll make food. But I want to take turns riding your dicks when you're done."

Trevino burst into laughter. "You can ride right now, Lil Baby. Fuck this weed; you're the ultimate high."

"Indeed," Bashir agreed, and they led her next door to the bedroom.

Chapter 6

Bashir

The perfect Valentine's Day gift for his loves was escaping Bash, and he was frustrated.

It was usually very easy for him to be creative, but trying to think of something Nasima and Trevino would both love was stumping him. He didn't want to skimp on his gifts; the past week and half had been about them learning how to move together as a loving polyamorous unit. Bashir needed his gifts to reflect how much he loved their situation, how much he wanted their relationship to continue forever.

He threw a jab into the heavy bag, dancing back on his heels and ducking left. He followed up with a right cross, moved around, landed a left hook and kept moving. He was up early sparring alone, the sun peeking over the horizon little by little as he worked out. Trev and Nas were snuggled up together still asleep; he had plans to wake them when his breakfast casserole finished baking. Bash continued his combinations, listening for the oven timer as he bobbed and weaved around the heavy bag.

"You only spar alone when you need to think. What's going on?"

Trevino's voice reached him, and Bashir turned, a smile on his face.

His love was standing in the doorway of the gym, scratching his toned belly, sleep still heavy in his voice. Five years later and Trevino Davis still took his breath away. Bashir thought it must be magic. Add Nasima to the mix and he was perpetually stunned and aroused by the wonder of them. It was pure sorcery.

"Morning, babe."

"Morning. You got me ready, in here all sweaty and sexy. But answer me, Butta. What's wrong?" Trevino came toward him, his shorts barely covering his monster of a dick, and Bashir licked his lips. But he should have known his baby wouldn't be deterred.

"I don't know what to get y'all for Valentine's Day," he confessed, knowing Trev wouldn't leave it alone until he told him. Trevino grinned.

"You up early, cooking and sparring—two things you only do alone when something's bugging you—for that? Butta, come on. You know me and Lil Baby will love whatever you do for us."

"I want it to be perfect. It needs to be something to let you know ain't shit changed in my heart for you, and something to let Nas know she's in my heart too now, but also something to tell you both how much I love us," Bashir explained. Trevino grabbed his arm, pulling him close. He kissed him softly, then started unlacing his gloves.

"As good as those things sound, it's a lot of pressure to put on a gift, Butta. And truth be told, I don't need anything to tell me ain't nothing changed. I came to our bed last night and you were there to hold me—like you are every night. I already know ain't nothing changed," Trevino said.

Bashir stared at him lovingly, his heart melting. Trev's slick ass mouth got him again. He let his man take his gloves off and wipe him with a towel. The oven timer sounded.

"Get our breakfast while I shower real quick," Bashir said, kissing Trev once more and going into the downstairs bathroom. He let the steamy water relax his muscles as he stood there, still contemplating the gift he wanted to share. As soon as he started lathering up, he felt a rush of cold air as the shower door opened. Hands snatched his sponge away from him and washed his back, the touch firm and familiar.

Trevino continued washing him, moving down to Bashir's ass and thighs. Bash moaned, dropping his head forward. Trev washed between his cheeks, then reached around and rubbed the soapy sponge over his dick and balls. Bash moved his hips, wanting more contact. His dick hardened, stretched, got ready. Trevino washed the rest of his body, steam from the water filling the space, the multiple jets ensuring they were both soaked.

"Trev," Bashir called out, needing his man's touch. Trevino put the sponge aside and pulled on Bashir's hips, widening his stance. Then he pressed on his back so he would bend. Bashir felt Trevino's fingers between his ass cheeks, then a thumb pressed inside him.

"We love you, Butta," Trev whispered, "and we'll love whatever you give us. Hear me?" Bashir nodded, moaning. Trevino pulled his thumb out and bent Bashir down more, making him brace himself on the bench. He heard his man fumbling with the lube they kept on the ledge next to their washing products. Trevino's fingers smoothed over his ass and inside, the lube cooling the way. Then Bashir felt Trev's dick push into his ass, slowly but steadily.

"Yes baby. Fuck me, Trev," he begged. Trevino grunted, easing his way inside. When his dick was fully embedded, he started to move. He reached around, grabbed Bashir's dick, and started rubbing and jerking as he fucked him.

"You mine forever, ain't you, Butta?" Trevino whispered, thrusting and breathing hard.

"I'll never give you up, Trev. I'll never let go," Bash promised, the pleasure clouding his senses. The feeling of Trevino's dick and hands was spinning him out of control. His moans got louder, more urgent. No one could love him like this man. He was completely sprung, every muscle attuned to the sound of Trevino's voice, the feel of his hands, the thrust of his wonderful dick. Bashir cried out, Trev's hands and dick bringing him closer and closer to the pinnacle of pleasure.

"Give me my nut, Butta. Your ass is so perfect and tight. Your dick is so fucking thick. I want your nut, Bashir. You ready to come? You gon give me my nut?"

"Yessssss," he yelled, coming so hard his eyes crossed, his sperm shooting out in thick rivulets. Trev pounded against his spot, and he kept coming, intoxicated by his man's dick in his hole.

"Oh shit, Butta. Fuck!" Trevino yelled, coming as well, emptying his monster dick in his ass. Bashir moaned, feeling weightless. Trev pulled out and helped him straighten up, turning him around and kissing him. Bashir kissed him back, his heart so full he couldn't speak.

Ten minutes later, they were both washed and out of the shower again, Trev getting back into his shorts and Bashir finding a clean pair of boxers and a t-shirt in the laundry room. When they reconvened in the kitchen, Nasima still wasn't down yet, but neither of them was surprised. They'd fucked her until she passed out the night before. Plus, since she'd been with them, no one required her to cook, so she always took advantage of her ability to sleep later. Trev started cutting up fruit to go with their breakfast casserole while Bash made toast.

Nasima came down as soon as they had everything ready, bonnet covering her hair, rubbing sleep from her eyes. She was in Trevino's shirt today and walking a little slower, a testament to how they worked her over the night before. She came to him, kissing his mouth and smiling at him.

"Why'd you leave us so early?" she asked him. Bashir held her close, smiling back.

"I needed a minute. No big deal," he replied. Nasima looked at him shrewdly, as if she wanted to question him further. Then she shrugged too, like she'd changed her mind.

"If it was something important, you'd tell me, right?"

"He doesn't know what to get us for Valentine's Day," Trevino said, eating orange segments while he waited for them. Bashir shook his head.

"Trev—"

"You weren't going to say anything so she wouldn't worry, but I could hear in her voice she was already worrying. So, I told her," Trevino said, cutting him off. He sighed, looking down at Nasima again. There was so much patience and adoration in her eyes, he was almost overcome.

"Oh, Bash. We'll love anything you give us. You know we will," she said.

"I want it to mean something, Lil Baby. Having you here is important, and special. I need to show y'all how appreciative I am, how happy this has made me," Bashir explained.

"Then don't overthink it. Because I already know," Nas said, winking at him. She wiggled out of his arms and went over to Trevino, snatching the bowl of fruit before it was gone. He scowled. She straddled his lap and kissed his frown away, holding his face in her hands. Bashir smiled. He grabbed the plate of toast and went to the table, sitting down.

"Now I was trying to let your pussy rest, Lil Baby, but you wanna be all over me. Get your ass in a chair before you get fucked and the food gets cold," Trev warned. Bashir laughed. Nasima pouted but moved to her own chair. Trevino kissed her soundly and started making a plate for her.

Bash looked around, seeing the rest of their lives play out in front of him. He thought of the perfect gifts. Satisfied, he took the plate Trev handed him and started eating.

Nasima

The next day, Nasima thought of her Valentine's Day gift for Vino and Bash while she was soaking in the tub, resting her sore muscles. Her body had never been worked with such sexual fervor, and she was feeling the effects. Not that her men weren't careful with her—they tended to care for her better than she did herself—but it was still more activity than she was used to. She'd been thinking of asking Bashir to teach her boxing, or at least some stretches. He and Vino were so limber, even with Bash being built heavier.

Nasima sighed, sliding deeper into the water. Bashir had poured rosewater and aloe vera oil into her bath, so she was feeling good and relaxed. Her gift was going to make them so happy. Plus, she planned to tell them she wanted to stay, so she was sure it was going to be a long night of love and lovemaking. Nasima grinned. She didn't pause anymore when she thought of them all being in love. She knew they were, and she knew it was real.

Coming home wasn't her first choice, but it was the best one, and her only regret was not finding her Vino sooner. She'd let Tone and Smoke get in her head, convince her she was out of options and Vino was lost to her because of Bash. Little did they know she was destined to have them both. And now she did. Nasima couldn't wait to see the look on her guys' faces when they saw her gifts, and when she told them she was theirs forever.

After her bath, Nasima dressed in black leggings, a long blue sweater, and boots. She and Bash left the house and headed to the gym so he could check in. Vino headed off separately to see King and handle some work; he promised to meet them later. When they got to the gym, Nasima sat on the side and watched everyone hard at work, fascinated by how much the feeling of peace permeated the place, even though everyone there was throwing punches. Bashir met with Linc and Bunky in the office, going over activities for the next week.

Her phone dinged with a notification. Nasima looked at it, a smile coming over her face. Her package had arrived at the mail center. It contained Bash and Vino's Valentine's Day gifts, and she wanted to get the box so she and Bash could take it home with them. She hopped up, going into the office.

"Bash?" she interrupted. Bashir looked up at her, smiling.

"Yes, Nas? You good?"

"I ordered something special, and it was dropped off at the mail center a minute ago. I'm going to get a rideshare and go get it, okay?"

"No, babe, I'll take you. Give me a minute," Bashir insisted. Linc and Bunky looked panicked. Nasima shook her head.

"It's clear you're needed here right now. I can go by myself. I'll be right back," she insisted. Bashir looked at her, his face a mask of worry. She sighed.

"I will call you when I get there and as soon as I'm on my way back," she promised.

Bashir sighed. Then he looked at Linc and Bunky, the open files on the desk in front of him, and the schedule on his computer monitor.

"Okay," he conceded, "but you come right back, Nas. I'm not playing. Trev is gonna kill me. You know how he worries."

"I won't tell him if you won't," she said, blowing him a kiss and smiling brightly. She skipped out of the office, using her phone to call a ride. Five minutes later, her ride was outside, and she slid into the backseat after verifying the driver and car.

"Two stops, right?" the driver said, and Nasima nodded. She knew her men would worry, but there was no better time to kill two birds with one stone.

After going to the mail center and getting her box, she had her rideshare driver take her to her cousin Smoke's house. She didn't have anything left there she wanted, and she wasn't coming back, but as her family, she felt she owed Smoke to thank him and tell him face-to-face. She got out of the car, assured the driver she wouldn't be more than ten minutes, and headed to the front door.

Her key didn't work, as she suspected; Smoke was petty enough to change the locks. Nasima knocked, hoping to get this over with quickly. Tone opened the door, looking wary.

He peeked behind her to make sure she was alone and then let her in, giving her a smirk.

"Look who it is, Smoke," he said, walking back into the living room as she followed. "I knew your ass would be back. You get tired of watching them two gay niggas suck on each other?" Tone cracked himself up, and Nasima shook her head.

He is such a clown, and a scary one at that, she thought, remembering the way he'd run out the back door the last time she was there. She wondered, for the millionth time, what she had ever seen in him.

Smoke was playing a video game with D-Wax, while Cameron smoked a blunt with two of their other friends. Candace was nowhere to be seen, but Nasima knew she was there. She didn't have a life outside of Smoke, plus some of the "friends" he invited over were other women, and she wouldn't leave Smoke alone with them.

"What you doing here, Nas? Whatever it is, make it fast. Last thing I need is to be any further on Truck's radar," Smoke said, impatience on his face. The areas around his jaw and eye were still slightly discolored. Nasima was sad. She hadn't wanted it to come to this. He was her only family; she didn't understand his need to treat her like a stranger on the street. She sighed.

"Fine, I'll make it fast. I came to say thank you. Staying here was a whole lot of bullshit, but you did take me in when you didn't have to. Thank you." As soon as she finished her sentence, Smoke and Tone stared at her, looking shocked and a little scared.

"Sounds like a goodbye," Smoke said.

"It is. I'm in a stable, happy place—a place I could have been in a long time ago if I hadn't let other people pull me from what I know is true. You won't have to worry about me anymore; it's not like you ever really did."

"So you thank me by shorting me? What about my money?" Smoke continued, scowling. Nasima took a deep breath, tamping down her feelings of guilt. Her first instinct was to offer him something, smooth things over, but she knew Vino would flip if he found out she'd given him more money.

"I think I paid enough, Smoke. I think you took enough from me. What you didn't get in cash, you got in meals. I did more than my part for this household," she said, holding her ground. She could hear Bashir in her head, saying he was proud, and she smiled a little.

"You really think those two freak ass niggas gon keep you around, Nas? You some kind of weird toy to them, and you gon be out on your ass again—"

"Don't talk about them. Keep them out of your mouth. And did you forget *your* friend is the reason I was out on my ass in the first place? I'd never have ended up back here if it wasn't for Tone."

"Wait a minute. I didn't—"

"You and the women you had sucking your dick for Percs lost me my apartment!" Nasima interrupted Tone before he could spew any lies. "You shouldn't even be speaking to me unless it's to apologize. I took your shit for so long because I believed you really wanted to make us work. But you only wanted to see how much you could get out of me. I hope you enjoyed what you did get because you're going to answer for it, trust me." When she finished, Tone shut his mouth, swallowing nervously. She knew he caught her meaning; he knew Trevino was the one he would answer to.

Smoke looked over at his friend, then back at her. "Nasima, don't start no shit. Tone is harmless, and you don't—"

"Was I the only one paying you?" Nasima interrupted him now, anxious to leave. She knew by now her men were on to her, and she needed to go to them before they came to find her. All she wanted was to hear the truth from her cousin's mouth. Smoke rolled his eyes and shook his head.

"I knew I could count on you to pay your part," he finally said. "Plus, Tone told me he was only back here cause of you; somebody had to pay for him." He shrugged after he finished, trying to appear as though he didn't care. D-Wax looked at her, ashamed, and even Cameron turned his face away. Nasima was sick to her stomach. And now she understood Tone's scared look when she said she wasn't coming back. Smoke would be a lot less tolerant of him without her money.

"You make fun of Vino and Bash's sexuality and you carrying a house full of niggas with no problem," Nasima pointed out. "You using Candace for her EBT and me for money and letting a bunch of grown men ride on your back? You sure you don't prefer them?"

Everyone's mouths dropped open as Smoke jumped up angrily. Nasima instinctively backed away. His face was a cloud of rage, his eyes narrowed into slits. He charged toward her with his fists raised. A shot rang out.

Nasima screamed and jumped as Smoke fell back, holding his bleeding thigh.

"I know you didn't have your fist raised to my Lil Baby," Vino said, entering the living room holding his gun. "I know you weren't about to hit her, not after I already told you I owed you a bullet the last time."

Smoke whimpered like a baby, writhing around on the floor. Candace ran in from the kitchen as Cameron and D-Wax looked for something to put pressure on the wound. Easy came in behind Trevino, his gun drawn as well, and everyone stopped moving. Smoke was crying as he held his bleeding leg, and Tone was shaking like a leaf. Vino massaged Nasima's shoulders and kissed the top of her head.

"Did he touch you?" he asked, looking around the room. Nasima shook her head.

"No, baby," she answered him. He turned her around, looked at her, and kissed her forehead.

"Go get in the car," he told her quietly, and she obeyed without argument, knowing she'd pushed his buttons enough for one day by coming here alone. When she got outside, Bashir was standing at his Range Rover.

"Your box is in the trunk. I tipped your driver, and he canceled out the ride," he said. Nasima went to stand in front of him, ashamed she'd lied to him.

"I should have told you," she whispered, reaching for his hands, "but I wasn't trying to come back. I want to stay with you. I thought I owed him a face-to-face conversation, that's all."

"Nas, do you know how much danger you put yourself in? I don't care about your little white lie, I care about you leaving yourself vulnerable like this. Me and Trev were losing our minds. Promise me you won't do this shit again."

"I promise, I promise," she rushed to reassure him. Bashir pulled her into his arms and sighed deep with relief. Trevino and Easy came out of the house, laughing and talking. Vino dapped Easy up and walked over to them. Nasima went into his arms next, but he didn't hug her back.

"Vino, is he—"

"Don't worry about him. Easy and the boys are taking care of him and Tone," Vino answered.

Nasima nodded, sighing. A small part of her thought it didn't have to come to this, but she knew better than to ask for any mercy on Smoke's behalf, especially after Vino saw him getting ready to hit her. She knew how Vino was coming behind her. How he always had.

"Okay. We're going home now?"

"In a minute because you not off the hook. Nasima Amara, you know better," he said. Nasima nodded, shamed again. He was angry with her.

"I do know better. But I thought it would be a good gift to tell you guys I handled this all by myself. I was going to surprise you and let you know I want to stay and tell you I stood up to Smoke. I thought—"

"Nas, you don't have anything to prove," Trevino said, cutting her off, "and when you walk into a house full of niggas who have already shown they will use you and don't care about you, all you're doing is scaring us. We know you're strong and capable, baby. We know you don't take no shit."

"But for fuck's sake, let us protect you," Bashir said, shaking his head. "We're your men. It's our job to take care of you. We ain't gon tell you no more."

"Okay," she agreed, letting her last barrier down, her heart pounding. Trevino said she would remember her power, and now she did. Her power was in her love, in her ability to summon support and protection whenever she needed it, in the way she commanded the hearts of these men. Her men. "I'm sorry. I'm so sorry."

Trevino finally returned her hug, kissing her hair.

"Get your stubborn ass in the car," he ordered, and she laughed, letting Bash help her into the passenger seat. Vino hopped in the back, and they headed home.

Trevino

"How did you find me? Y'all tracking my phone or something?" Nasima asked as soon as they got in the house. Trevino looked at Bashir, and they both laughed.

"Naw, Lil Baby," he said, hanging his coat and taking Nasima's to hang it as well. "We'd never track your phone without telling you. Our relationship has to be about trust or it ain't gon work. Butta called me as soon as you left and told me you were off on your own. I sent the watcher to watch, and he told me where the car took you."

"Easy snitched on me?" she asked incredulously. Trevino laughed again.

"Fuck yeah. You went into Smoke's house with no backup. I know he's your cousin, but none of them niggas can be trusted."

"How much of the conversation did you hear?" she asked next.

Trevino sighed. He'd heard pretty much everything, and his heart broke a little for her. Smoke was supposed to be her family, the only family she had left. But he knew what she was really asking. She wanted to know if he'd heard the things Smoke said about him and Butta.

"I heard enough, baby. And everybody in there heard me. Both Tone and Smoke will be taken care of, soon."

"Are you meeting up with Easy to handle them yourself?" Nasima asked, her voice small and scared. She knew what Truck Davis was capable of; she knew Trevino leaning into the violence his work demanded was a darkness no one escaped from. Trevino laughed.

"I'm not even getting into Truck mode for them bitches. Easy and the boys got it. I didn't even tell them how to finish it; I want to see what they come up with," he said, shrugging. Bashir nodded, proud of him.

As much as Trevino wanted to avenge Nasima's pain, taking things into his hands when he was so attached wasn't a good idea. Truck Davis was the best because while his skill was engaged, his heart was disconnected. Romelo was his cousin, but what he did for him was business. He'd never remain detached thinking of how they'd hurt Nasima, which could make his violence spill into something uncontrollable. He didn't want to go there; he might not make it back.

"Y'all wanna eat?" Butta asked. Nasima grabbed both their hands and headed for the stairs. Trevino stopped her, forced her to face them. She was breathing hard, her whiskey eyes filling with remorse and lust.

"Lil Baby—"

"I was a bad Lil Baby today and I need to make it up to you," she whispered. She headed up the stairs and they followed, immediately under her spell.

When she got to the bedroom, she pulled off her sweater, throwing it onto a chair. Trevino was right at her back, unfastening her bra and tugging it off her arms. Nas turned to face him, her soft titties pressing into him.

"I'm sorry," she whispered.

"Show us," he whispered back.

Soon, they were naked on their huge bed, Nasima on her hands and knees, taking his dick in her perfect pussy from behind while she sucked Butta's dick into her mouth. They held hands above her, their rhythm hard and slow. The men savored the pleasure moving through them, leaning forward to kiss, their tongues wrapping around each other.

Nasima was a masterpiece, taking them so well, her moans and whimpers letting them know she loved the way they gave her their bodies. Trevino smacked her ass, watching it jiggle and bounce while he fucked her. Butta had his head thrown back now, his hands tangled in Nas's hair, his mouth open in ecstasy. Trevino felt wetness as Lil Baby released, her thighs quivering, her pussy gushing. She moaned, her mouth full as she sucked Butta's dick even harder. Trevino picked up speed, slapping against her ass with his body, feeling his balls tighten. Lil Baby's pussy was gripping him as she came, and he was almost gone.

"Shit, shit, shit," Butta cursed and then groaned, long and loud. Nasima moaned again too, working her jaws, and Trevino knew she was swallowing Butta's nut. She sucked so long he had to pull out of her mouth and push her head away so she'd stop. Trevino smirked. She be wearing his ass out, he thought. He refocused and smacked her ass again, fucking her hard and fast.

"Why you go over there by yourself, Lil Baby? I was losing my mind, worried over you," he demanded.

"Vino, I'm sorry, baby," she cried out since her mouth was free. "I won't be bad again!"

"You ever scare us like this again, we're not fucking you for a week, you hear me? We taking this dick away. Is that what you want?"

"No, baby," she protested on a moan, "please don't take it away."

"You better learn your lesson then," he bit out, his head spinning, his nut ready. "Now come on this dick."

Nasima obeyed instantly, screaming out her pleasure and wetting him all over again. Trevino was right behind her, coming so hard his vision blurred in front of him. Nasima fell onto the bed, and he fell on top of her, drained. They crawled up to Bashir and wrapped around each other before falling asleep.

Valentine's Day
Nasima
The three of them slept late and made love as soon as their eyes opened. Bashir and Nasima made brunch and presented Trevino with his own large bowl of fruit to enjoy while they cooked. After food, they relaxed. Trevino and Bashir got up to go spar, and Nasima knew it was time for her gift.

"Wait!" She stopped them, going to drag the box from the closet. "I have to give you my gifts now." She got the box and sat it in front of the two of them.

Bashir opened it, pulling back the packaging bubbles and paper. The two of them stared down, shocked into silence. Nasima got them both custom gloves and head guards in yellow and black, embossed with a lightning rod. Trevino's set had "The Enforcer" written on them, while Bashir's read "The Foundation."

"Nasima," Bashir said, his voice heavy with emotion.

"Do you like them?" she asked, nervous. Trevino pulled her close and kissed her mouth.

"Lil Baby, this is amazing," he said. Nasima smiled.

"Vino, you're the Enforcer—not because of your work with King but because you're our protector. You keep order in our world. Bash and I can be anything we want to be because you make it safe. Bash, you're the Foundation because you make our home stable. You keep us whole. I feel like a queen because my castle is steady and protected. Happy Valentine's Day."

"You know you ain't going nowhere, don't you, Lil Baby?" Bashir said, pulling her over to him. He kissed her hard. Nasima nodded.

"I'm never leaving you," she promised. Her men raved over her gift and pulled her into the gym with them, eager to try it out. The sparring was more playful than serious, but they loved the new gloves and head guards. They especially loved how she came to them after, handing them a bottle of lube, and whispered, "You looked so good, so sexy. I want you both inside."

When they got to their bedroom, Vino and Bash took turns kissing her mouth, stopping in moments to kiss each other while rubbing her breasts. Soon, she was lying between them, their mouths each full of her nipples, their fingers intertwining as they played in her pussy together. Nasima moaned, cried, and came all over their thick fingers in a passionate rush. The double stimulation was unraveling her fast, and all she wanted was more. The air crackled with lust and love, hummed with their joy in being together and exploring each other's bodies. Nasima's hands reached to rub her men's chests, their stomachs, her nails digging in when the pleasure took her too fast.

"I—oh shit, please—"

"What you beggin' for, Lil Baby?" Bashir whispered. "We about to give you everything you want."

Nasima whimpered, her body shaking. Vino's fingers were inside her now, hooking gently, caressing her spot. Bashir's circled her clit, pressing and stroking. The pressure built, and she closed her eyes. The world exploded and a scream escaped, surprising Nasima. Her pussy creamed, pulsed, and released the fluid of her rapture. She felt a million tiny lights behind her eyes, felt fireworks in her body. It was one of the best orgasms of her life. But her body still hummed, thinking of her men and their thick dicks, waiting for her. She needed more.

"You need a break, Lil Baby?" Vino asked, finally unwrapping his lips from her nipple. Nasima shook her head, her senses ablaze. She wanted them inside.

"Not yet. Not until you fuck me—please fuck me," she said, still a little breathless. Vino and Bash looked at each other, nodding. Vino laid flat on his back and gestured to her.

"Come get on my dick, baby," he said, grabbing her. Nasima sat up and got into position, her dripping pussy wetting the head of his dick. She sank down, her mouth open, soft cries pushing out of her as she took inch after inch into her body. As soon as she was full, Vino brought her down until she was lying flat on top of him. Bashir got behind her, spread her ass cheeks, and licked her from her hole to where her pussy lips were quivering around Vino's dick.

"Oh shit," Nasima said, the feeling unfamiliar but enjoyable. Bashir's tongue pushed into her hole, wetting the area, then swooped down, sucking her pussy lips and licking at Vino's dick. She kissed Trevino, moaning into his mouth as he moaned back, starting to move underneath her and thrust gently.

Bash put some lube on his fingers, rubbed it around her asshole, and pushed inside. Nasima gasped, her body shaking a little. It wasn't painful, but it was an adjustment. Vino was still fucking her from below, and Bashir was kissing on her ass cheeks, rubbing and caressing them.

"Relax, Nas," he coaxed her, "I got you. I'm right here." He added another finger and Nasima moaned, the double penetration sending her spinning. A little more lube and Bash was three fingers deep, stretching her hole while she rode Vino's dick slowly. Vino growled, mumbled about her good her pussy was, promised to eat it for the rest of his life. Nasima kissed him, capturing his tongue, heightening the sensations for them both. Bashir removed his fingers and coated his dick with lube, getting into position atop her. He opened her ass cheeks and pressed forward, the head of his dick stretching her anus. Nasima tensed and whimpered.

"Relax, mama," Vino coached her, still kissing her mouth between sentences. "You're gonna feel pressure, and maybe some pain, but you'll adjust quicker if you relax. Look at me, love. Focus on me. Butta loves you so much, Lil Baby. He'll never hurt you."

Nasima nodded, took a deep breath, and relaxed her muscles. Bashir moaned, pushing further inside. When he was halfway in, he stopped so everyone could get their bearings. Vino kissed Nasima and rubbed her back, calming her. Bashir rubbed her ass, kissed her spine, and promised to be gentle.

"I love you, Nas," Bashir whispered for the first time. Nasima came, her orgasm surprising them all, her body jerking. Bash took the opportunity to slide himself into her ass fully, and the three moaned at the same time. Bashir and Vino got into a rhythm, fucking her both ways, only the walls of her pussy and ass separating them.

"Oh, baby, oh yes," Nasima sobbed, the passion overtaking her, the feelings vibrating all over her body. These men belonged to her, and she to them. They'd made a home for her, with her, and now inside her. She loved the way they moved together, praised her body, praised each other, and made their enjoyment known. She'd never felt so complete. Vino grunted, letting her know he was finally close, and Nasima praised God for her man's stamina as she adjusted. Bashir moved in her ass, growling his pleasure.

"You so good, Lil Baby. So fucking good," he bit out, trying to keep his pace steady so as not to hurt her. Nasima moved with them, double-filled and spinning into the clouds, her body barely her own anymore.

"Take it all, Lil Baby," Vino said. "It's yours. Our good girl is taking all this dick, ain't you?"

"Yes—oh, yes. Bash, I love you too. Vino!" Nasima cried out, coming hard, tears running down her cheeks. The grip of her pussy urged Vino right behind her, and he spilled himself inside her with a groan, kissing her mouth and cheeks. Bashir thrust into her hole once, twice more and pulled out abruptly, coming on her ass in thick spurts. He dropped to the bed beside them, closing his eyes. Nasima looked at him, smiling fondly.

"You be wearing his ass out," Vino said, chuckling. Bashir grunted, still unable to move. Nasima giggled, feeling worn out herself. She relaxed on top of Vino, content.

After, the men showered and ran her a bath with soothing soaking salts for her exhausted body, then they changed into lounging clothes. Bashir got them all t-shirts that said, "I'm With Them," and as corny as Vino thought it was, even he put his on. Then Bash brought out his real gifts. Handing each of them a box, he gestured to open them.

Nasima opened hers first. It was a brand-new laptop, top of the line, engraved with *TNB* in script and the words, "The Breath of Vino and Bash." She squealed, loving the new computer, but also loving their claim of her.

"Lil Baby, you're the wind lifting us, the breeze calming us, the beauty of the sky and the heavens right here with us. You're the air between us, Nasima. You make all this possible," Bashir said. Nasima started to cry, moving her gift aside and throwing herself into his arms. Bashir held her, whispered words of love, and thanked her for giving him a chance. Nas held tight, her heart bursting with lust and love and appreciation. She wiped her face and turned to Vino.

"Open yours," she told him. Trevino had a much smaller box, and he opened it quickly, pulling out a hand-engraved pocketknife with a blue steel blade. The handle was embossed with the words, "Protector of Butta and Lil Baby." It was sleek, elegant, and exactly Trevino's style. His grin was wide.

"Butta, this is dope. Thanks, babe," he said, smiling so big. He leaned over to kiss Bashir, and Nasima watched, loving when her men were affectionate and carefree. After the second round of gifts, everyone was hungry again. Bashir ordered Indian food and they all watched TV. Then there was a knock at the door.

Trevino got up to open it, taking a package from a messenger. He came back to the couch, opening the package. He pulled out two velvet boxes, looking inside to verify before handing one to each of them. As with Bashir's gift, Nasima opened hers first. It was a gold link chain with a "Lil Baby" charm in the middle. She laughed.

"Vino, this is so you. I love it," she said. Trevino laughed too. Bashir opened his box. It held a matching chain with "Butta" on the charm in the middle. Bashir grinned.

"Look at you, collaring us. Everybody gon know who we with, huh?" he joked.

"You better know it," Vino said back. He helped Nasima fasten the chain around her neck and kissed her lingeringly, his lips soft and sure. He kissed Bashir as well and then gathered them both to him on the sectional.

"We got it right this time, Butta," he said. Bashir nodded. "We did."

"I got it right too," Nasima added. "I was afraid when you asked me to stay, when you said I was the one. I didn't know what to expect. And I thought this would disappear. But something pulled me into you and kept me here. I listened to my heart, and I stayed, even though I was scared. And now I'm more in love than I could ever imagine being. I got it right too."

Her two men looked at her with so much love in their eyes she was emotional.

"We got you, Lil Baby, and you got us," Trevino whispered. "And now we can all breathe easy."

Chapter 7

Epilogue

Three Months Later

Trevino

Trevino took a deep breath, relaxing his muscles. Bashir's hard dick eased inside his lubed-up hole, and he moaned as the tightness gripped him. Trevino sighed, adjusting as he felt the tendrils of pleasure surrounding him. He didn't bottom often—in fact, before Butta, he never did at all—but his loves' desires trumped any insecurity, and he wanted them to know he was open to satisfying them in whatever way they wished.

"Trev, you feel so good," Butta said, still moving slowly, anxious to be inside but determined not to hurt his lover. Nasima was underneath him, her thighs open to his face, her eyes wide and filled with lust.

"Vino, you look so beautiful," she whispered.

Trevino smiled and then moaned as Butta filled him up. When he was fully inside, Bashir took a breath, massaged Trevino's ass, and waited a moment. Trevino grabbed his own dick in one hand and leaned forward until his breath was moving the hairs on Nasima's pretty ass pussy. She spread wider for him, one thigh over his shoulder with her ankle dangling, the gold anklet wrapped around it with a boxing glove charm reflecting the light and throwing shadows on the wall. His name was tattooed on that same ankle, permanently inked since they were eighteen, in the same script as her name etched over his heart.

Trevino growled, pressing a kiss to her plump pussy as Butta started to move. Feeling his man so deep was intoxicating and Trevino's tongue snaked out, pushing between Nasima's lower lips and tasting her honey. She whimpered, her back arched off the bed, and she grabbed for his head. The three of them fell into a wonderful rhythm, Trevino's licks and slurps becoming deeper and longer as Butta moved in and out, picking up speed. Nasima sang his name as he tasted her, and he let her cries set the tempo for his hand around his own dick, pulling and sliding. In and out, tongues and dicks, Butta's guttural moans and Lil Baby's scattered sobs. Trevino was in heaven, loving that he was filled with the both of them and they were filled with him.

"Gotdamn, Trev. I—fuck, you feel amazing."

"Vino, Vino—shit, shit, shit!"

Trevino listened as his loves moved toward complete satisfaction, and he moaned louder into Nasima's pussy, heading there himself. His Lil Baby was riper, sweeter than ever, and Butta's dick hit him deep and hard, driving him to the edge. Trevino jerked his dick harder and felt his balls tighten. They were almost there, and he knew they'd come together. Nasima's cream glided onto his tongue, and he lapped it up greedily, glancing at her face. Her eyes were closed, and her fingers were wrapped around her own nipples, pulling and tugging, heightening her pleasure. Trevino sucked her clit harder, dragging his hand up and down his shaft, twisting at the head of his dick. He was so fucking close.

"Yes, yes!" Butta exclaimed, thrusting with abandon, heading to his paradise. Two more thrusts and he was coming, pulling out and painting Trevino's ass with his nut.

Trevino's own nut burst forth, coating the palm of his hand. He cursed and yelled out, the sound muffled by Nasima's pussy. Trevino continued licking and she screamed, her pussy pulsing, her cream oozing onto his tongue. He consumed every drop of her, addicted to her taste. Nasima writhed and shook, trying to get away from his relentless mouth.

"Vino, I can't—baby, please," she begged, her body sensitive to his touch. Trevino ignored her, devoured her, made her come again and again.

Bashir was finally able to stand and went to the bathroom, coming back with wet cloths and towels. Then he got beside Nasima, whispering in her ear and kissing her cheek. Only when she was a quivering, crying mess did Trevino finally lift his face. He crawled up her body and kissed her mouth.

"You okay, Lil Baby?" he asked. He fell on the bed beside her. Nasima nodded, turning into his arms.

"You drive me crazy, Vino," she mumbled. Bashir laughed. He turned her back and wiped her down, then tossed Trevino a towel. Trevino cleaned himself up and reached out, pulling his family close.

"Lil Baby seem different to you?" Trevino asked Butta as they undid their gloves after sparring the next day. Bashir stared at him, his face confused and curious.

"Different how?" he asked.

"I don't know if it's me, but for some reason, she's more...lush, I guess is the word. Her skin is softer, her pussy is wetter and sweeter. Hell, she even comes faster. And her fucking scent? It be calling me. As soon as I walk in this door, I'm heading to her."

"It's not just you," Butta confirmed with a smirk on his face. "I've been trying not to look like a horny dog humping her leg, but every time I see her, I need to feel her."

"Exactly. Something is up."

"You think she's pregnant?" Butta said.

Trevino let his gloves fall to the floor. He stood there, surprised into silence. When Nas moved in permanently, she realized she'd left her birth control at Smoke's house, and they'd taken her to the doctor to reup. So, of all the things, he'd never considered that.

"Why would pregnancy cross your mind? Lil Baby's on BCs," he asked. Bashir shrugged and bent to pick up Trevino's gloves.

"They're not a hundred percent, Trev. And it's a good explanation for everything you're describing. Her scent and taste being riper, her pussy running wetter—could be the hormones, all of it."

"Shit, you're right. Nas might be pregnant. Well, what—I mean, should we say something to her?" Trevino asked, tiny frissons of fear running through him. Most of him was excited by the possibility of finally being a father. He wanted as many babies as Nas was willing to give them, but he didn't want a repeat of the past—for either of them.

"Trev? Where'd you go?" Bashir asked, and he snapped out of his reminiscing and tuned back into the conversation.

"I'm sorry, babe. What were you saying?"

"I was saying we should let Nas come to us," Butta repeated, staring at him. Trevino nodded in agreement. He knew Butta wanted to know where his memories had taken him, but he couldn't tell him. This one thing...it was only for him and Nas.

"You're right. We don't want her to feel overwhelmed. And I think she trusts us enough to know she can come to us with anything."

"Right. We'll wait for her. Hey, Trev? You good?" Bashir pressed him, still staring.

Trevino nodded again. He was good. But he needed Nasima to be good too.

Nasima

Nasima got out of bed, stretching her body. Moving into the bathroom, she showered quickly and moisturized her skin, then went into the closet, looking for something to wear.

She and her loving, incredible men were going to barbecue in the backyard. Spring had arrived and the weather was perfect—cloudless skies, soft breezes, and gentle sun. Easy, his girlfriend Keona, and their son, EJ, were coming over too, as well as Romelo and his two ladies, Bibi and Sadie. Bashir said Linc and Bunky might stop by after the gym closed, but they weren't confirmed. Nasima decided to wear her favorite red joggers and a cropped white tee with a black graffiti design. She grabbed the items, marveling again at how efficiently Bash fit her clothes into this closet. He'd moved their lounging and sleepwear (because it wasn't like they ever wore it anyway), as well as Trevino's work clothes into the room closet next door, and brought her clothes in.

Nasima dropped the outfit as well as her socks and underwear on the bed and went back into the bathroom. She took a deep breath and pulled the box with her pregnancy test from its hiding place under the sink. Then she shut the door and locked it, wanting to have this moment alone.

Seventeen Years Earlier
"Vino, we need to talk," Nasima said, entering his apartment.

Her best friend and only love was sitting at his kitchen table, looking at a map and taking notes. His cousin Romelo was gaining more and more respect from the higher-ups, and they'd finally promised him his own territory. The catch? He had to devise a takeover plan himself. So, twenty-year-old Romelo brought in the one person he knew he could trust—his seventeen-year-old cousin, Trevino.

Romelo knew Trevino was smart and would know how to plan and anticipate. Plus, he understood people. No one could see the big picture like he could. Nasima was often in awe of his mind. He'd aced math and social science classes all through school and even graduated a year early. She wished her Vino would use his extraordinary genius on something else, but she knew he wouldn't leave Romelo hanging, and no one was more at home in these streets than he was.

"What's wrong, Lil Baby?" he asked without looking up. He addressed her as he always did, and Nasima felt his love all over her. Trevino continued making notes while he used one long arm to clear the chair beside him. He patted the seat and gestured to her. Nasima sat down next to him, kissing his cheek. He smiled and turned to face her, kissing her mouth with so much passion she reached for him.

"How is it going?" she asked him. Trevino shrugged.

"It's going. We need a targeted attack on these two blocks at once; these niggas are soft, so it'll be easy. The other side of the alley will fall in line after we're done. None of them like leading, and they'll be happy to collect their money and have somebody tell them what to do," he explained, pointing at the map and showing her what he was speaking of.

"Sounds like you're in business."

"Melo's in business, baby. I already told him if I help, I want to be on enforcement and protection. I ain't gon be no corner boy and I ain't gon manage them. Somebody else can do that shit. Now, what did you need to talk about?"

"Vino, I'm pregnant." Nasima dropped the bomb before she could lose her nerve. She stared at her man, hoping against hope he'd be happy and not angry or regretful. She knew seventeen was early to start a family, but she also knew she and Vino were forever. Trevino stared back, his eyes wide. Then, he grinned.

"Seriously? My Lil Baby is having my baby?" he said. Nasima nodded, and he pulled her close, hugging her so tightly she could barely breathe.

"You're not upset?" she asked. He pulled back and looked at her, shaking his head.

"Hell no. You're my life, and we're having a baby. I know it's soon, but I'll take care of you, Nas, I promise."

"I know you will, baby. We're going to be fine," Nasima said, her happiness finally pushing through. Now that she knew Vino wasn't upset, telling her parents would be a breeze.

"When I finish this, we'll go and get your stuff—"

"My stuff? Why?"

"Lil Baby, you've been resisting moving in with me since I got this place. I let you make it cause I know you feel like you can't abandon your parents. But I'm not about to have my baby in that type of environment," Vino said.

Nasima sighed. It was no secret her parents were more concerned with getting high than with being parents, but his words still hurt. And no matter what, they were her mom and dad. It didn't feel right abandoning them.

"Vino, I—"

"This ain't a negotiation, Nas. You're moving in with me, end of story," Vino said. Nasima scowled.

"You can't decide for both of us and then refuse to talk about it. You promised we would find our way together. What I want matters too, Vino!"

"Of course it does, Lil Baby. But I know how you get behind your parents—staying up all night trying to keep them in the house, cooking and cleaning up after them and their high ass friends, scouring the streets for them when they disappear. It's not cool, and you ain't doing it with my baby inside you. And don't think I don't know you use the money I give you to pay back people they scammed or burned. You ain't doing that shit no more either," Vino said, looking into her eyes.

Nasima looked away, ashamed. She did a lot of clean-ups where her parents were concerned, not wanting them to meet the fate of the addicts no one cared about. It weighed on her, but they were all she had, and she wasn't ready to give up yet.

"You can't tell me not to be there for my family; look at what you're willing to do for Romelo," she shot back at him, frustrated. Nasima knew their situations were different because Romelo treasured and appreciated Trevino's loyalty and repaid it in kind, but it was the only argument she could come up with. Vino sighed and shook his head.

"Nas, I'm not doing this with you. You know it's not the same. I don't know why you won't let me care for you—why *you won't look after your own heart for once. I'll protect you with my life, you know I will. But our baby—"*

"Give me three months," Nasima said, grabbing his hand. Her heart pounded in her chest. It was time to look out for herself and the baby growing inside her, but she needed a little more time. She'd stay with her parents a little longer and then she'd go. "I promise I will come here and let them fend for themselves in three months. I need time to try to get them some other support, and time to...say goodbye."

"Ninety days, Nasima Amara," Vino agreed, kissing her hand and holding it to his chest. "Three months, and then it's our family from here on out."

Nasima nodded, her heart bursting with love even though she knew there would be hard times ahead.

Nasima woke up from her daydream about the past and stared at the finished test. Two pink lines. Pregnant. She swallowed, feeling slightly nervous. This was real, and it was time to tell her guys.

Bashir

Bashir was more convinced than ever his theory was correct after he watched Nasima nurse the same glass of wine the entire cookout and never drink from it. It confirmed not only that Nas was pregnant but that she knew it too. She was slick enough that no one else noticed, but he and Trev stayed in tune to her, so he saw it and knew his man saw it too. He hoped she was ready to talk about it because he was excited at their family expanding, though he knew it was soon.

He was an only child, born to a couple who had no real desire to be parents. They were moderately successful businesspeople who traveled as much as they could and pretended they didn't have a son until someone forced the issue. He'd spent most of his childhood in the house where he currently lived with his lovers, being raised by his paternal grandmother. Their connection was why Bash ended up being her sole beneficiary when she died, which was still a sore spot for her son, Bash's father, even after all these years.

Bashir used to dream of making his own family, of having children who would never have to wonder whether he loved them. Of finally being in a place he could belong. He met Trevino and knew it wasn't out of the question. Adoption would have been part of their overall plan if Nas wasn't a part of their lives. But she was, and now they were having a baby. Bashir grinned. He couldn't wait to kiss and hug Nas, sink inside her, celebrate this new life with her. He could practically smell her already.

"Butta, what you dreaming about over there?" Trevino said, locking the gate as their last guest left the yard. Bashir snapped back into reality, looking at the empty trash bag he was holding in his hand. Nasima giggled, looking up from gathering the domino set and the playing cards from the picnic table.

"Whatever it was, it must have been good. You haven't even opened the bag," she pointed out. Bashir grinned sheepishly and opened the bag in his hands, walking around to pick up trash. With the three of them working, the yard was spotless, grill cleaned and leftovers put away in record time.

Nasima headed upstairs first, coming down clean and smelling fresh, wearing socks and a t-shirt. Trevino used the first-floor bathroom and grabbed a pair of boxers from the laundry room. Bashir started the dishwasher and copied his lovers, showering and coming back to the living room in a pair of sweatshorts. The three of them snuggled on the couch, watching a documentary.

"I have something to tell you," Nasima said from her spot between them. Bashir stared down at her, then up at Trevino, his heart speeding up. He loved these two so much.

"What's wrong, Lil Baby?" Trev asked, looking down at her as well. Nasima sighed.

"I'm...pregnant," she said softly, like she was afraid of their response. Bashir grinned. He'd known it was true, but hearing her say it was still a heady moment. Trevino kissed her hair.

"Are you okay with it? Are you happy?" he asked. Nasima nodded, her smile growing.

"Yes. I am very happy. Please be happy too," she said. The two of them hugged her tightly, kissing her mouth, neck, and cheeks until she was breathless.

"Of course, we're happy, Lil Baby," Bashir said, "but we thought you were taking something."

"I stopped six weeks ago," Nasima explained. "I hate the way they make me feel, but in my previous situation, there was no way I could get pregnant, so I put up with the side effects."

"We're glad you stopped," Trevino said, "you shouldn't be taking anything making you feel bad. And we're so happy about the baby, Nas. It's all we've ever wanted."

"How are you feeling? You need anything?" Bashir said, running his hands over her body. His sweet, precious Nas —their gorgeous fat mama—needed the best care, and he would make sure she got it. Nasima giggled as his hands tickled her.

"I feel fine. I'm hungrier than anything, I've noticed. I need to make a doctor's appointment to confirm. I think I'm at four weeks, but I want to keep this between us until I'm in the second trimester."

"Of course, baby. We'll do whatever you want, and we'll take you to the doctor tomorrow," Trev promised. Nasima leaned up, searching for his kiss. Trevino pressed his lips to hers, closing his eyes. Bashir felt like there was something on both their minds, something from their past he wasn't aware of. He wasn't upset, but he worried about the memories that seemed to be surrounding his two loves.

"Vino," Nasima said, reaching back for Bashir's hand, "it wasn't anyone's fault, you know that. This time is not last time, and Bash is here with us."

"Okay, Lil Baby. I got you. This time is not last time," Trev said. He looked up into Bashir's eyes. Bash was surprised at the pain he saw there. He looked down at Nasima, and her eyes reflected it.

"What happened?" he asked. Nasima sighed so deeply.

"I knocked Nas up when we were seventeen," Trev started, rubbing Nasima's shoulders. "She was still living at home with her parents, and I was about to help Melo take over his first set of blocks."

"My parents were addicts, and I was a codependent who wouldn't leave them. When I told Vino I was pregnant, he wanted me to move in with him and stop doing so many risky things to protect them. I made him give me three months. Three months to separate myself from them and untangle so I could focus on the baby. But I went right back to trying to save them, and it was so much stress."

"And I wasn't paying attention to her because we were taking over those damn blocks. I wasn't checking in with her like I usually do. A week from the deadline, I went out of town with Romelo, told Nas we'd move her when I got back," Trev continued.

"My parents went on a binge, and I was out half the nights looking for them—"

"Which I never would have allowed if I'd been there," Trevino interrupted.

"Vino came home just in time for me to miscarry," Nasima choked out, her words almost a sob, tears running down her cheeks. "All I wanted to do was hold him and apologize. But he kept apologizing to me. Can you believe that? He blamed himself for not being there. We both felt awful. It was...it took a long time to be normal again."

After she finished speaking, Bashir felt so many emotions running through him. Sweetness and love because Nas and Trev trusted him enough to share something they'd obviously been keeping for the two of them. There was pride because they'd managed to salvage their love and keep their hearts unguarded. But also, sadness at the pain and guilt they were holding onto, and a fierce need to protect them from ever experiencing the same kind of pain again.

"This time is not last time," Bashir said, moving in close and wrapping them both in his arms. "I'm so sorry, my loves. It was an accident, and neither of you are to blame. But this is now, and I'm the foundation, remember? Nas, you're never alone, and Trev, you don't need to look after her all by yourself. Our home is stable, and there's no stress. We're going to have nine months of good food, good love, rest, and happiness. And then we'll have our baby. We got this. And I got y'all."

"Bash, I love you," Nasima said, burying her face in his chest. He felt her tears and rubbed her back, holding her tightly. Trev leaned over and kissed him, their tongues tangling. Bashir felt his heart pound, his chest tighten. These two were his entire world.

"Butta, you're everything," Trev whispered when he lifted his head. Nasima pulled back from his chest and Bashir kissed her too, sharing Trev's flavor with her.

When everyone was calm, he got up and went to the kitchen, coming back with a tray of sandwiches and snacks. The three of them watched television and munched happily, with both Bashir and Trevino stopping to rub Nasima's belly and talk to their baby. After the food, they all snuggled together with blankets over them. Bashir looked down at Nasima's big breasts as she lay against him, dozing off. He chuckled softly.

Trev lifted his head. "What's so funny?" he asked.

Bashir grinned. "I was just thinking...if you think she tastes good now, wait until she has milk," he replied, pointing down at Nasima's chest.

Trevino's eyes went wide, and he looked at their woman with hunger in his gaze. Nas started, waking up and shifting her body.

"Don't even get it in your head," she mumbled, "my milk is for our baby."

"Butta, you need to research how to encourage more milk production," Trev said, shifting so he was using Nasima's breasts as a pillow, "cause that little nigga is definitely sharing."

Bashir burst into laughter and held his family close.

Sneak Peek- Her Solid Ground

Welcome to Coming Home: The Elements Series.

Coming Soon- Her Solid Ground

Elliott Joseph "Easy" Tanner was a quiet and observant man, most times choosing to watch instead of speaking, always patient and willing to wait for the right moment. And he'd thought he found it with Keona Mikayla Ross. Their love was the perfect balance; she was the bright spark to his quiet nature, a firecracker to his silent sky. And then two years ago, she left without an explanation, breaking his heart. Now Keona's back, with eyes full of fear, and secrets. But she's as quiet as Easy about what drove her home. Can he get the truth out of her? And when he finally knows everything, can they pick up where they left off?

Chapter One
Keona

Keona Mikayla Ross slung her tote bag over her shoulder and carried her three packed duffle bags out to her car, the old Volkswagen she'd first arrived in. She was hardly allowed to go anywhere, and was driven when she did, so no one would be looking for this car. Once everything was loaded, she went back into the house, looking around one last time. Then she went into the library, pulled a book by the spine, and watched the wall shift away. Her father's safe came into view. Keona put in the combination, swinging open the door and peering in. The safe had a few stacks of cash, and a small wooden box; the rest was paperwork and bonds. Keona grabbed one of the stacks of cash and the wooden box, opening it and removing a gold locket. Elliott had given it to her, and it was the first thing her father took away. He'd kept it to remind her of his threats whenever she dared get out of line.

Satisfied that she wasn't taking anything that could be used to track her, she went to her bedroom to get the one thing she couldn't leave behind. She leaned over the bed and scooped up her sleeping child, kissing his face and rocking him gently. The baby fussed a little and settled down again, drooling against her shoulder.

"Time to go, Lil Man," she whispered in his ear, grabbing his favorite stuffed animal and his blanket, "Time to go see Dada."

Keona left the house and put her son in his car seat. She hopped into the driver's seat and started the car, looking back at the luxury prison she was leaving behind. It was a quick look, because the security camera reboot would be finished soon and everything would be working again. She turned on the radio, letting the low instrumental music play a soundtrack to her thoughts. She'd make her first stop in a couple of hours, to change her son, get them both some breakfast, and see if she could find a prepaid cell phone. Keona sighed. She had to use her time wisely. Her father wouldn't be home from his trip for another week at least, which meant she had a week to get to Elliott, tell him about their son and convince him to keep EJ safe while she got further away. The thought of leaving her sweet baby gave Keona pains in her chest, but his father was the only one she could trust. She didn't expect Elliott to protect her too, not after the way she'd left him, and not with her suddenly reappearing with the son he never knew about. If he took their child, it would be enough for her. She'd manage the rest on her own.

Two hours later, Keona pulled into a rest stop. Her son, Elliott Joseph Tanner the Third, or "EJ" was awake and whining, ready for milk. Keona parked at the far end of the lot for privacy, got into the backseat with her baby, took him out of the chair and lifted her shirt, cradling him as she popped a breast into his mouth. EJ sucked greedily, his eyes closing and his little jaws working. Keona sat back against the seat, sighing deeply. She'd been trying to wean him gently, but now there was no help for it. She would have to pump as much as she could before she left and hope EJ adapted quickly. Two tears fell down her cheeks and Keona swallowed, trying to stay under control. Tears wouldn't help her now. Once EJ was safe with his father, and she was far away, then she would cry.

Keona left the rest stop after using the bathroom to freshen her and EJ, getting them both an egg sandwich, and buying some essentials, including some ready made food, spring water, a prepaid cell phone, and some snacks. Hours passed, and finally Keona pulled into a motel in her hometown. She used cash to rent a room for three nights; she didn't figure she'd need more than that to convince Elliott to keep their son. Once she was in the room, she took a quick shower while EJ slept, fed him half a sandwich and nursed him, then played with him and his shape toys until he fell asleep again. Keona got into bed beside her son, holding him close. She thought of his father, her only love, the man she'd most likely made an enemy of by walking out on him without an explanation and disappearing with no contact. Keona sighed.

She hadn't accepted things being over with her and Elliott; she always hoped one day he'd be able to forgive her. But this wasn't the time or the situation to ask that of him. It was too much, and their family deserved better. They deserved a real chance to try, not a rush to forgiveness because she was in trouble. Keona didn't bother wiping the tears falling onto her cheeks this time. She missed her man, and was about to miss her baby. Maybe it was time to cry after all.

The next day, Keona got dressed and had breakfast quietly. She didn't need noise anyway; her thoughts were blaring and intrusive, like a TV when you've lost the remote. EJ woke soon after her and she fed him some cereal, played with him and then gave him a small dose of cough syrup and nursed him into his mid-morning nap. He was getting over a little cold; but the syrup was mostly so he'd sleep a little longer. She left the room, locking it behind her, and got into her car. Keona had a sick feeling in the pit of her stomach, leaving EJ alone. But there was nowhere to take him. Hopefully, she wouldn't be too long.

When she pulled up in front of Elliott's three-story town-house, memories flooded back with a vengeance, twisting up her stomach even more. Keona chose this house with him. She decorated, picked out their furniture, and made love to Elliott in every single room to welcome them home the first night. This was *her* house too. She took a deep breath, trying to get her stomach and bowels under control.

"Just do it, Key," she whispered to herself, "It's not for you, it's for EJ. Get out of the damn car." After another deep breath, she opened the door, exiting the vehicle. She hurried to Elliott's front door, not giving herself time to get nervous. Keona pushed the doorbell once, twice, her fingers shaking. After a moment, she could hear someone coming down the stairs. The first level was simply the garage and Elliott's office—there was nothing beyond the front door but a small entryway with the stairs to the upper level, and another door on the side that led to the garage. Keona heard a surprised gasp, then the click of the locks and the door was yanked open.

"What the hell are *you* doing back here?" Laney Childs, once her longtime friend and confidant, looked at Keona with an angry sneer. Keona was surprised, but fixed her face to mask it...and the hurt. What the hell was she expecting? For Elliott not to move on? She was disappointed it was with someone she'd thought of as her friend, but reasoned that the two of them probably bonded through their shared anger. After all, she'd left Laney without a word too.

"Laney? I didn't know—never mind. Look, I need to speak to Elliott. Can you ask him to come down?"

"*Easy* doesn't want to talk to you, and neither does anyone else. Go back to wherever you came from, Key. It's too late."

"I know you're upset with me, and you have a right to be, but—"

"I'm not upset, baby girl. You showed me what you thought of our friendship and I'm matching your energy. As for Easy, he's very well taken care of, so like I said, you can go," Laney spat out, her frown deepening. Keona took a deep breath, tried to be calm. But the old Keona was brimming under the surface—the one who swung first and talked later. The one who didn't let anyone give her shit, or question her place, especially where Elliott was concerned. She balled her fists, counting to ten. This is for EJ, she reminded herself. She could take it, for EJ.

"You can hate me later, Laney. This is an emergency. I need to see Elliott, right now," she insisted. Laney sucked her teeth, and propped one hand on her hip.

"And I said he don't want to see you."

"Okay, I don't have time for this. I can apologize as much as you want later, but you need to move, before I move you. You know I don't have a problem throwing hands, Laney. Just like you know I don't play about my man."

"*Your* man? Bitch—"

"Yo Laney, what the fuck? I told you to let whoever it was in on your way out, not argue in my fucking doorway. Why —Keona?" In the midst of their push and pull, the owner of the house jogged down the stairs, stopping short when he looked into her eyes. Elliott Joseph Tanner, II. Her love. The man who was once her life. The streets called him Easy but she never had; she left his nickname for his friends, his work associates, for the women who wished he'd been as deep in their guts as he was in hers while they were to-gether. She left his nickname for the people who couldn't see inside his heart, who couldn't read his soul. To her, he was Elliott—always had been, always would be.

He looked the same, his six foot two frame towering over her five foot six one with ease. Elliott was slender, his body unassuming, but he was strong and his muscles were defined; he'd lifted her thick ass many a night in their bedroom. His skin was the color of hickory, a shade past syrup, almost carob but not quite. And his eyes were huge —big and round, almond colored and always open. That's why they called Elliott, "The Watcher." He was the most observant person she knew, and his eyes never missed a lie. Keona was counting on that. It was how he would know she was telling the truth about EJ. Those eyes went into a beautiful wide nose and full mouth and Keona was in love as she looked at him over and over again. Her heart never wavered for this man. But now, his full mouth was twisted in a scowl as he waited for her to speak. She swallowed nervously.

"Yes, it's me. Hi Elliott. I'm sorry to come here like this, but we have to talk. I need your help."

"My he—my help? That's what you have to say to me? You only here because you need something from me?" he yelled. He moved closer, outside now, and Keona backed away from his anger, wondering if she'd made a mistake. Maybe I hurt him too badly, she thought.

"Exactly. Coming back here, slumming because you want a favor—"

"I told you I don't play about my man, Laney. Mind your fucking business!" Keona exploded, turning to her ex-friend. Confronting Elliott might make her nervous, but confronting another bitch *about* him was never an issue. She turned back just in time to see a ghost of a smile on his face. He remembered how she got down. Keona's spirits lifted. Maybe she hadn't ruined everything after all. Laney stood there in shock, anger coming off her in waves.

"Easy, are you gonna stand here and let her—"

"Honestly, this is a lot in front of my door and I think both of y'all need to go," he said, sighing deeply. Keona clasped her hands together, getting desperate. She had to make him understand.

"You're sending me away? She's the one who doesn't belong here," Laney said.

"Elliott, please. I need five minutes. I have to talk to you. It's an emergency," Keona begged, unashamed. She was past her pride. This was about EJ.

"Laney, you don't belong here, either. You told me what you came to tell me, now leave. Keona, I don't know what you want, but the answer is no," Easy said, sounding tired and sad. Laney stomped off to her car, but Keona remained, her eyes wet and stinging. He turned to go back inside.

"Elliott, baby please—"

"Key, stop it goddammit. I don't care what you need—"

"I need you to take care of our son!" she called to his back. Elliott stopped. He turned, his big eyes on her...staring into her soul.

Acknowledgements

Jaleesa Jackson- Who always ALWAYS mentions my name, and is first in line to support my work. I love you, friend.

Kimmie Ferrell- Who pulled me back in when I wasn't sure. You saved me, and helped create this. You're stuck with me now, lol. Love you.

A.K Edits- It's nice having you on my team.

The Chary Assist- Cover Queen. Thanks for keeping me calm and helping me loosen up.

Natasha Bishop- Watching you shine has inspired me in ways you don't even know. I love you!

A.H. Cunningham- Your willingness to push the boundaries of what we think makes a love story has given me so much courage. I'm proud to know you. Love you!

Torri- My baby baby (she gets two babies, lol). I love you so much. Thanks for all your insight.

About The Author

Shameka Erby is a writer from Philadelphia currently living in Baltimore. Her love affair with romance novels started early, and she loves writing sweet and sexy love stories. To date, she has written ten romance novels and three short story collections. Her work has been featured in Brown Sugar Literary Magazine, Stuck in Notes Magazine, and on websites such as Permission to Write, Oyster River Pages, and Raising Mothers. Besides her fiction works, she also publishes nonfiction essays on Medium and has a newsletter, Just A Girl and Her Laptop.

Find her work here: www.shamekathewriter.com

Twitter and Instagram: @Shamekawrites

TikTok: ShamekaTheWriter

Books By This Author

The McNeal Love Stories
The Driver's Seat
Find My Way Back
The Officer and the Butterfly
The Greatest Risk

The Royal Romances
Hooked On Your Love
Until You Come Back To Me
All I Need
Don't Play That Song
The Going Away Present: A Mal and Luchi Short
Love Notes: Sexy Holiday Stories

Short Story Collections
Accessories of Love
Heartbreak Alley
Blood Ties